The Bobbsey Twins and the Circus Surprise

By

LAURA LEE HOPE

GROSSET & DUNLAP
Publishers   *New York*

PRINTED IN THE UNITED STATES OF AMERICA

The Bobbsey Twins and the Circus Surprise

CONTENTS

CHAPTER		PAGE
I	MISCHIEF MAKER	1
II	CALLING ALL CARS	11
III	A CIRCUS CHILD	21
IV	THE EGG HAT	30
V	AN ELEPHANT'S SURPRISE	40
VI	BERT TO THE RESCUE	51
VII	A COOKHOUSE LUNCH	62
VIII	LIONS!	74
IX	SHADOWY FIGURES	82
X	MISSING!	91
XI	FAT-LADY FLOSSIE	100
XII	A LAUGHABLE EXPLOSION	109
XIII	FREDDIE A HERO	118
XIV	A FUNNY MIDGET	128
XV	A TIGHT-ROPE CAT	138
XVI	A WELCOME VISITOR	147
XVII	FOUND!	158
XVIII	THE BEST REWARD	172

CHAPTER I

MISCHIEF MAKER

"I SEE some customers!" blond, blue-eyed Freddie Bobbsey said excitedly, looking down the street. "Orangeade! Orangeade—five cents a glass!" he yelled hopefully.

"It's only Bert and Nan!" said Flossie, who was Freddie's six-year-old twin and looked much like him. She waved to her twelve-year-old sister and brother, who also were twins.

When Bert and Nan reached the juice stand, Flossie handed each of them a paper cup of ice-cold orangeade.

"This is good," said Nan, smiling. Like her twin, she was slim and had dark hair and eyes.

"Hits the spot!" Bert declared. "Here's a dime."

"Thanks," Freddie said. "This will help our project." He noticed a poster tucked under Bert's arm. "What's that?" he asked curiously.

Bert grinned. "Something super!" he exclaimed. "The Happy Top Circus is coming to Lakeport!"

"The circus!" Freddie cried happily. "Yippee!"

"Goody, goody!" Flossie danced around the little stand.

Bert turned the poster about. Animals, clowns, and bright-colored balloons flashed out at them. Flossie and Freddie read the bold black type:

THE HAPPY TOP CIRCUS
COMING TO LAKEPORT FRIDAY, JUNE 18
FEATURING A SPECIAL EVENT—
THE JACK HORNER PIE
COME AND SEE WHAT'S IN IT!

Lakeport was the town where the Bobbsey twins and their parents lived in an attractive, three-story house. A short distance away was lovely Lake Metoka, on which Mr. Bobbsey had his lumberyard and sawmill.

"I got the poster from Mr. Butler at the drugstore," Bert explained.

"It's bee-yoo-ti-ful!" Flossie exclaimed. "And circuses are the most fun! But what about the Jack Horner Pie—do you know what's in it, Nan?"

"No, I don't," her sister admitted.

Bert chuckled. "Neither do I. We'll have to see the circus to find out."

Flossie thought a moment, then said, "Maybe

the pie has something to do with the nursery rhyme."

"You mean about the boy who put his thumb in a pie and pulled out a plum?" Nan asked.

"That's right," Flossie nodded.

"Well, I don't think so!" Freddie spoke up. "Everyone knows that rhyme. 'I'll bet this is a chocolate-cream surprise pie!'"

The other children laughed, for the chubby little boy was always hungry.

"Perhaps the circus ticket-taker will give everyone who comes in a piece of pie," Bert said teasingly.

"Oh boy! I'm going to buy lots and lots of tickets!" Freddie said eagerly.

Nan looked at Freddie with pretended dismay and made up a rhyme:

> "Little Freddie Bobbsey
> Sat in a corner
> Eating some circus pie—
> An elephant walked by
> And gave a loud cry—
> Saying 'Freddie Bobbsey
> Is fatter than I!'"

"Oh, Nan!" Freddie protested, but the other twins laughed until their sides hurt.

When they stopped laughing, Freddie begged Bert to tell more about the Happy Top Circus.

"It's a good-sized one," Bert said, "and tours the country in trucks. Mr. Butler says most of them will arrive in Lakeport on the night of June 17, and the circus men will set up the equipment the next morning."

Flossie sighed. "That's so long! Five whole days to wait!"

"Where did Mr. Butler say the circus tents are going to be put up?" Freddie asked.

"In the large empty lot near the park," Bert replied. "Near the Lakeport shopping center."

Flossie's face lighted up as she said, "Don't you love the elephants—and—tigers—and clowns—and music—and—"

"And little monkeys like you and Freddie!" Nan concluded as Flossie paused for breath. Then she sat down on the grass beside Bert.

Flossie poured cups of orangeade for everyone. "This drink is free," she told Nan and Bert. "We didn't want to charge you before 'cause you're in the family. But we need all the money we can earn."

"For what?" Bert asked.

Freddie said that a summer camp for needy city children was being built outside Lakeport. It was to be called "Campers' Corner." Teddy Blake, one of Freddie's playmates, had told him and Flossie about it that morning.

"We want to buy bathing suits for two campers—" Flossie said. "One for a girl and one for a boy."

"Sounds neat!" Bert said. "A new camp will

need all kinds of equipment and games, too."

Nan turned to her twin. "Maybe you and I can think of a way to earn money. I wonder who the head of the camp is? We could speak to him and see what the campers will need."

"Teddy heard it was a man from out of town," Flossie spoke up. "But he was leaving Lakeport today, and won't get back until just before the camp opens."

"When is that?" Bert asked.

"The fourth of July."

"Well," Bert said, "we have the rest of this month to raise money. When the camp director comes back, we can give it to him."

"Won't he be surprised!" Freddie exclaimed.

"Now that school's out, we have lots of time," Flossie said. "But how can we earn money besides selling orangeade?"

"I have an idea!" Nan said. "We can give a circus of our own. Home circuses make lots of money and everyone loves them."

"That's terrific!" Bert said. "But maybe no one will want to see it after going to the Happy Top Circus."

Nan thought that if some of their friends were in the acts, their friends' parents and relatives and neighbors would certainly want to see them perform. "Besides," she added, "we could have our own show the end of this month—long after the Happy Top leaves here."

"I guess you're right," Bert agreed, warming to the plan. "We'll need at least two weeks to get ready. Where will we give our circus though?" he asked.

"How about the big vacant lot behind our garage?" Nan suggested. "We can ask Dad if it'll be all right."

"And Flossie and I can set up our juice stand there," Freddie said. "People always get thirsty at circuses."

Flossie giggled. "We'd better start squeezing oranges now so we'll be sure to have enough juice for lots 'n lots of customers!"

The discussion was interrupted by a joyful bark from the Bobbseys' dog Snap. The large, shaggy-haired white pet trotted across the street toward them.

"Over here, boy!" Freddie whistled, and the dog obeyed. He was panting from the heat.

Jokingly Nan held up the circus poster. "Look, Snap!" she said.

The dog barked twice and sniffed at the sheet. "Snap remembers the circus!" Freddie said proudly.

Several years before, Snap had been in a trained dog act with a circus. But now he had to be urged to do his tricks.

Flossie poured some orangeade into a saucer and set it on the ground. "Here, Snap," she invited, "this will make you feel cooler." Eagerly, the Bobbsey pet lapped up the juice.

Meanwhile, Freddie counted the money he and Flossie had collected. "Thirty cents—" he was saying when Snap suddenly growled.

Nan looked down and cried, "There's a hornet on the saucer. Hold still, Snap!"

But Snap growled again. With a loud

Bzzzzzzz, the black-and-yellow hornet flew onto his nose and stung him! Snap yelped with pain, then leaped up. As Snap fled into the road, the twins saw a car zooming toward their pet.

"Snap! Snap!" they screamed.

Scree-ch!

The car was almost upon the dog, but Snap had stopped in his tracks when the driver slammed on his brakes. As the man opened the car door, Snap crept back to the sidewalk, his tail between his legs. Flossie comforted the frightened dog while Freddie rubbed some moist mud on Snap's swelling nose.

Bert and Nan walked over to the driver, who had a pleasant face, bright-red hair, and lively green eyes.

"I'm glad I didn't hit your dog," he said. "My name's Riker. I've been searching the neighborhood for my own dog, Chips. He seems to be lost.

"I'm on my way out of town," Mr. Riker explained. "I stopped at a gasoline station a few blocks back and Chips jumped from the car window. I thought I saw him head for this block. He's a black-and-white fox terrier."

"We haven't seen a dog like yours around here," Bert said, "but we'll look for him." Bert introduced his sisters and brother, then suggested that Mr. Riker search other streets in the neighborhood, while they looked in nearby gardens. "You can call us later, if you don't find him. We're the only Bobbseys in Lakeport."

"Thanks," the man said. "I'll do that. If I don't find Chips, I'll certainly check back with you."

After Mr. Riker had driven off, the twins

looked back of every house on their street, but there was no sign of the terrier. Finally they went into their own home.

"Let's call our friends about giving a circus," Bert urged.

The twins took turns at the phone. They found the other children eager to take part in the back-yard circus to make money for Campers' Corner. They promised to discuss details later.

Flossie and Freddie decided to return to their orangeade stand. As they sat down on the grass, the small twins heard a shrill whistle. They looked to their right and saw a heavily built boy of Bert's age ambling down the sidewalk toward them. He was wearing blue jeans, a white shirt, and an orange baseball cap.

"Danny Rugg!" Flossie whispered.

Danny was a bully, who frequently played mean tricks on other children. He had caused trouble for the Bobbsey twins many times.

Danny drew closer and surveyed the little stand. "Well, well!" he sneered. "What do you know—orangeade!"

"Would—would you like some?" Flossie asked.

"Yeah," he replied. Freddie poured a cupful. Danny gulped down the juice.

"That'll be five cents, please," Flossie told him.

"Says who?" Danny mocked.

"We do," Freddie spoke up staunchly. "We're selling this orangeade."

Danny gave a scornful laugh. "Five cents for that stuff? Tastes like water mixed up with fake food coloring. I'll bet it is!"

"That's not true!" Flossie protested angrily. "It's made from fresh oranges."

"You owe us a nickel!" Freddie declared.

Instead of paying, Danny gave the wooden stand a hard kick. It toppled over. *Crash!*

CHAPTER II

CALLING ALL CARS

AS the orangeade stand crashed to the ground, Danny Rugg ran off, leaving Flossie and Freddie staring with dismay at the damage he had done. The glass pitcher had fallen to the sidewalk, and had shattered into tiny pieces. Pennies, nickels, and dimes were lying in an orange puddle on the grass.

"What a mess!" wailed Flossie.

"You—you mean old bully!" Freddie cried.

Just then Snap, barking angrily, bounded up to the twins. "Come on, Snap!" Freddie urged, starting after Danny.

The older boy had stopped running and was looking back to see if he were being followed. Snap gave a ferocious bark and raced ahead of his young master. Freddie knew that Snap would not injure the bully, but would give him a good scare.

11

"Get him, Snap!" Freddie urged. But Danny fled with amazing speed. A second later he turned the corner and disappeared.

"Halt!" Freddie commanded Snap. The dog lay down at the boy's feet, panting. "You scared him, anyway," Freddie said, patting Snap's head. "Let's go back."

Freddie found Nan and Bert helping Flossie sweep the debris from the sidewalk into a dust pan. Bert said he and his twin had heard the

crash and come outside to see what had happened.

"Danny made a getaway but he's plenty frightened!" Freddie said proudly.

"Swell!" Bert spoke up. "I'd like to find him —and punch him in the nose!"

Flossie looked worried. "I'm afraid Dinah won't like it 'cause the juice pitcher we borrowed is broken in teeny bits."

Dinah Johnson was the jolly colored woman who helped Mrs. Bobbsey with the cooking and housekeeping. Dinah's husband Sam worked for Mr. Bobbsey at the lumberyard. The couple lived on the third floor of the Bobbsey house and were a beloved part of the family.

Nan reassured Flossie, saying Dinah would surely understand that the mishap had not been the twins' fault.

Freddie remained disconsolate as he said, "Well, even if Dinah isn't angry, we're still out of business—the grass drank all our orangeade!"

Bert laughed. "Nan and I will help you make more next time you set up the stand," he promised, handing Freddie the coins he had picked up from the ground.

As Freddie took the coins, a station wagon turned into the Bobbseys' driveway. "It's Mother and Dad," said Nan, and the twins ran to greet their parents, who got out of the car laden with bundles.

"Can we carry something?" Freddie asked, catching a tiny package which slipped from Mrs. Bobbsey's grasp.

"Thanks, dear." His mother, slim and attractive, hurried toward the kitchen door. Over her shoulder she added, "And there's a black bundle in the back seat of the car which belongs to you and Flossie."

Curious, the young twins hurried to the automobile, and Flossie opened the rear door. She giggled.

"Snoop!" she exclaimed, and reached inside for the family cat. Snoop was all black except for a white streak underneath his chin.

"So this is where he's been hiding all day!" Freddie said, as the pet snuggled down in Flossie's arms with a contented purr.

"Snoop was playing stowaway." Flossie laughed merrily.

Meanwhile, the older twins had put away the wooden stand and safely disposed of the broken glass. The children met in the kitchen where Mr. and Mrs. Bobbsey were talking with Dinah. The plump colored woman asked Flossie and Freddie, "Did your juice business turn out all right?"

With sad expressions, the small twins told how Danny had upset their stand.

"That dreadful Danny Rugg!" the cook exclaimed. "But never you mind 'bout the broken pitcher, honey lambs—it was just a cheap one."

The twins' parents were also indignant at the bully's mischief-making, but decided to make light of the matter.

"I'll help you build a sturdier stand, Freddie," Mr. Bobbsey offered, "and nobody will be able to knock it over. We'll glue it to the sidewalk!" he joked.

Bright smiles broke out on the children's faces. "You're all nice as—lollipops!" Flossie cried.

Freddie grinned. "Lollipops! I'm so hungry I could eat a dozen."

Dinah chuckled. "You'd better not. Supper's almost ready."

Later, when the family was seated in the dining room, Dinah carried in a chicken, roasted golden-brown, with peas and fluffy mashed potatoes.

"*Ummmm,* our fav'rite meal," Flossie declared.

As Mr. Bobbsey served, Freddie asked, "May I have the wishbone, Daddy, so I can wish circus day to come sooner?"

Mr. Bobbsey nodded, and said, chuckling, "So you've already heard about the Happy Top Circus."

"Yes. Please may we go?" Flossie begged.

Mr. and Mrs. Bobbsey laughed, confessing that they had already made plans for the family to attend the Lakeport performance.

"Oh goody, goody," cried Flossie.

Nan, her eyes sparkling, turned to her parents and said, "We have some more circus news. We're going to put on a little circus ourselves in a couple of weeks to make money for Campers' Corner."

"Sounds like a worthy project," Mr. Bobbsey commented. "It will take a lot of work."

"Oh, all our friends are going to help, and do different tricks and stunts besides," Nan said.

Excitedly the twins discussed plans for their show. Mr. and Mrs. Bobbsey exchanged glances, pleased at the children's desire to aid less fortunate youngsters. Dinah, serving dessert, listened approvingly.

"I'm sure," she said, "you all will be dandy— 'most as good as the Happy Top."

"Thanks, Dinah." Nan smiled. "We hope you and Sam will like it."

The family had just finished eating, when they heard a thumping noise in the kitchen and Dinah's excited voice saying:

"That's the boy! Hit it hard!"

Everyone hastily left the table and rushed into the kitchen. A strange and amusing sight greeted them. Dinah was keeping time with her feet as a small, black-and-white terrier beat its tail against the bottom of a roasting pan. Dinah, after washing the pan, had placed it on the floor, intending to put it away in a lower cabinet.

Rat a tat tat! Rat a tat tat the animal's tail was beating as it struck the roaster.

Dinah shook with laughter. "He's a one-dog musical band!" she exclaimed.

Mrs. Bobbsey asked how the animal had entered the kitchen. Dinah said that a few moments before, she had opened the back door to let Snoop out, when the strange dog rushed up the steps past her and scampered inside.

"Isn't he cute!" Flossie cried, walking over to pet the terrier.

As she started to do this, the animal leaped high in the air and landed on the floor again, giving a swish with his tail. Then, with bright eyes, he barked as if waiting for applause.

The children clapped, and Freddie said, "You're a very smart dog! Too bad you're not ours. You could teach Snap that trick."

Bert and Nan immediately thought of Mr. Riker and his lost fox terrier. "But this dog can't be his, because the man said he'd come back and tell us if he didn't find it," Nan concluded.

Her twin went over to examine the dog's collar. There was no name plate on it.

"I guess you're right, Nan," Bert said. "This is somebody else's dog."

Mrs. Bobbsey suggested that Dinah give the animal something to eat and let him outdoors to return to his home. The cook offered the terrier a small steak bone. With a pleased yip the frisky little animal took the treat. The small twins wistfully watched him bound down the back steps and out of sight.

The others walked into the living room, where Mrs. Bobbsey said she planned to go to the Blaine farm the following morning for fresh eggs, butter, and vegetables.

"You mean the farm outside Lakeport where they have Shetland ponies?" Bert asked. His mother nodded, and the older twins asked if they could go with her.

Just then Flossie and Freddie burst into the living room.

"Suppose," Flossie asked, wide-eyed, "the name fell off the dog's collar and he doesn't have any home to go to!"

Bert snapped his fingers. "You could be right, Floss. Why didn't we think of that before?"

Nan gasped. "Let's hurry outside," she urged. "If that *was* Chips, he may still be around."

"I'm sure he can't have gone far," Mr. Bobbsey remarked, adding with a smile, "All cars on the lookout for a waggy-tailed dog chewing a Bobbsey steak bone!"

The four children scoured the neighborhood, but to their disappointment the terrier was nowhere around. Flossie and Freddie were crestfallen. To make them feel better Nan and Bert told the small twins about the pony farm they would visit the next day.

Early the following morning, Mrs. Bobbsey and the children headed for the Blaine farm in the family sedan. After driving for fifteen minutes, they reached an old farmhouse which was built near a grove of tall evergreens.

"Isn't it lovely!" said Nan, admiring the red and yellow roses banking the driveway.

After the car was parked, the Bobbseys walked to the kitchen entrance and rang the doorbell. A moment later a gray-haired, pink-cheeked woman opened the top half of the Dutch door.

"Why Mrs. Bobbsey!" she exclaimed. "How nice to see you—and these are your children?" After being introduced she said, "Come in, come in—you've arrived in time for a snack. I just baked a pecan coffeecake."

"Um, thank you!" exclaimed Freddie.

While they ate the coffeecake and had large glasses of fresh milk, Mrs. Bobbsey gave her order.

"I'll tell my husband about the vegetables," the farmer's wife said. "But Sandra's the chief egg-gatherer this summer. Perhaps you children wouldn't mind looking for her outdoors—"

"Who's Sandra?" Flossie asked.

"My granddaughter. She's visiting me."

The twins said they would be glad to look for the girl, and Mrs. Blaine pointed toward a large red barn a short distance from the kitchen door.

"I think Sandra's behind the barn."

The children thanked Mrs. Blaine for the snack and walked outside. Each had the same idea. This might give them a chance to see the ponies!

"Sure wish we could have a ride," said Freddie.

The twins reached the back of the red barn. Nan, who was in the lead, stopped short.

"Oh—look!" she cried.

CHAPTER III

A CIRCUS CHILD

AT Nan's cry, the twins looked in the direction she was pointing. A hundred yards away, near the bottom of a sloping hill, was a small ring enclosed with a neat white fence. Inside the ring a girl was performing fancy tricks on the back of a Shetland pony.

"A bareback rider!" exclaimed Bert and Freddie in unison. Nan nodded, eyes intent on the girl.

Flossie, however, looked puzzled. "What's a bear-back rider?" she asked. "That girl is riding a pony—not a bear!"

The children chuckled at the way Flossie had mixed up the word "bareback." Bert said that a bareback rider rode a horse or pony without a saddle. It was very hard to do.

"Oh!" Flossie exclaimed admiringly. "She must be a real smart girl."

"I wonder if she's Sandra?" Freddie asked.

"Let's find out," Bert suggested, and the twins walked toward the pony ring.

The young girl was so intent on doing a somersault on the pony's back that she did not notice the children's approach. Suddenly, however, Freddie stepped on a dry twig. *Snap!*

Startled, the bareback rider turned around and seeing the Bobbseys cried out, "Hello there!" Then, "Whoa, Cockles!" she commanded the pony.

"Are you Sandra Blaine?" asked Nan, as the animal trotted over to the fence rail.

"Yes, I am!" the girl replied, as she hopped off Cockles' back and jumped from the railing to the green grass surrounding the ring. "But my friends call me Sandy," she added.

The pretty girl had light reddish-blond hair. Tiny golden freckles were sprinkled over her face and arms. She looked about ten years old.

She grinned at the Bobbseys. "Don't tell me!" she exclaimed. "You're twins!"

Bert laughed. "You're right," and he introduced the visitors. "Say," he continued, "you're a swell horseback rider."

"Thank you. I've had lots of practice," Sandy replied with a modest smile. "Is there something I can do for you?"

Nan explained that they had come for eggs, and Sandy said she had left the egg baskets in the barn. She invited the twins to accompany her while she got them.

"Oh, yes," Flossie said eagerly as she hurried to walk beside Sandy. "And will you tell us how you learned to back-horse ride?"

Freddie, Nan, and Bert also looked at the girl with interest while waiting to hear about this. A sad little expression flickered briefly in Sandy's green eyes.

"Well . . ." she said, as if in doubt. "I guess there's no reason not to." Then she smiled. "Of course I'll tell you. I learned to ride in the circus, but I almost hate to talk about it now."

"The circus!" shouted the small twins in unison. At their cry, Sandy grinned, and Nan explained about the Happy Top Circus.

"I hope I can go to it," Sandy said as they entered the red barn and seated themselves on a pile of soft hay. Then she began telling the twins her story.

"Most of my life has been spent under the big top. You know that means a circus tent," she explained. "My mother and father were aerialists, and did tricks on the high-wire."

Freddie's eyes were round as full moons as he said, "Isn't that dangerous?"

"Yes," Sandy admitted, "but circus performers try to be very careful. My folks were one of the best high-wire acts in this country."

Sandy continued, saying that her mother was called "Rusty" because of her auburn-colored hair, and her father "Red," for his was a bright shade.

"Where are your parents now?" asked Nan curiously.

Sandy's face fell. "Mother's in a hospital out West and Daddy's looking for a new job," she said sadly.

"Oh, I hope your mother will be all right!" Flossie said with sympathy, and the other twins echoed this.

"Mother's getting better," Sandy replied. She explained that her mother had fallen from an insecure high-wire during a circus performance a month before. She had injured a leg badly but it was mending now.

"The circus had to move on," Sandy continued, "and Daddy decided to send me to Gramp and Grandma for a while. You see, Mother won't be able to do the high-wire act any more. And

Daddy has to look for other work because at the circus they were a team."

"That's too bad," Freddie said at once. Then he suggested, "Maybe your dad can find a job with the Happy Top Circus."

"That's an idea," said Sandy. "Oh, if only he were here! Daddy promised he would let us know when he found a job. I certainly miss my parents," she sighed wistfully. "But I'm lucky to have super-special grandparents!"

At that moment Sandy's grandmother called from outside. "Where are you, Sandra?"

Sandy picked up an egg basket and dashed outside, followed by the four twins. Mrs. Bobbsey stood talking to Mrs. Blaine and a jolly-looking man of about sixty.

"This is Gramps!" Sandy said proudly, and introduced Mr. Blaine to her new friends.

The farmer was dressed in overalls and a blue-plaid shirt. He was packing ripe red tomatoes, green beans, and garden-fresh lettuce and carrots into wooden baskets.

"Hello, children!" he said, and the twins grinned up into his cheerful face as they returned his greeting.

"And now I'll get the eggs," said Sandy, as Bert offered to help Mr. Blaine carry the filled baskets to the car. When this was done, the farmer invited the Bobbseys to take a look around his property.

"May we see the other ponies?" Freddie asked eagerly.

"And have a ride on one?" said Flossie.

Mr. Blaine replied that Cockles was the only pony left on the farm. "I recently sold the others to a riding-stable owner," he explained. "But I kept Cockles when I learned Sandy would visit us."

Seeing the disappointment on the small twins' faces, Mrs. Blaine said that Sandy would be happy to give them a ride on Cockles later. Flossie and Freddie immediately cheered up.

The farmer led the Bobbseys around the barnyard. First they went into two other large barns which were very clean and orderly. Then he took them through several sheds and smaller buildings where farm machinery was kept. Finally he pointed to a row of stalls near the red barn.

"These are for some of the smaller animals," Mr. Blaine explained. "Take a look."

The twins and their mother peered into the first stall. A beautiful collie dog lay there with four little puppies sound asleep at her side.

"I gave Lady and her puppies to Sandy when she came to stay with us," the farmer explained.

In a muddy pen nearby, a fat sow grunted loudly. The mother pig looked as though she intended to protect her litter of pink babies, and no nonsense about it.

Freddie exclaimed, "I'd like to take a baby pig home with us!" and looked hopefully at Mrs. Bobbsey.

His mother threw up her hands in pretended dismay. "What will you think of next?" she asked, and everyone laughed.

As the group moved on, Nan caught up with Mr. Blaine. She told him about the Happy Top Circus coming to Lakeport. "Sandy would love to see it," she added.

To Nan's surprise the farmer's face became grave. "Please don't mention it to her," he asked. "The less Sandy hears of the circus, the better it will be."

"But—but—" Nan stammered, about to say that Sandy already knew.

Her explanation was interrupted as her mother called from behind, "Has anybody seen Flossie?"

Nan looked around with surprise, for she had thought that her younger sister was walking beside Mrs. Bobbsey. But Flossie was not in sight. The group craned their necks for a glimpse of the little girl.

"Where could she have gone?" asked Nan, puzzled.

"Maybe Flossie went back to look at the lambs," Bert suggested. But Flossie was not near the stalls.

Everyone cried out "Flossie! Flossie!" but got

no reply. Mrs. Bobbsey looked very worried.

"Maybe she wandered into one of the vegetable fields," suggested Mr. Blaine, and he and Nan rushed off to search. But the fields appeared deserted.

Mrs. Bobbsey went to look through the barns again. Bert turned to Freddie. "Maybe Flossie's talking to Mrs. Blaine in the house. Let's find out."

As the two boys neared the kitchen door, they saw Sandy Blaine walking toward it. The girl was carrying two filled egg baskets. "Have you seen Flossie?" Bert called to her anxiously.

Sandy stopped short and looked at Bert with surprise. "Why, didn't you know?" she replied, "Flossie's at the hen house."

"You mean up there on the hill?" asked Freddie, glancing toward a low white building on a narrow slope beyond the farmyard.

Sandy nodded, explaining that Flossie had joined her there a few minutes before. She wanted to see the baby chicks and had begged to remain in the coop while Sandy returned to the house.

Relieved, Bert gave a loud whistle which summoned the other searchers. Nan, Mrs. Bobbsey, and the farmer rushed up, and Bert told them about the discovery.

"Thank goodness!" Mrs. Bobbsey sighed.

Mr. Blaine suggested that the other Bobbseys

visit the hen house also. "It's divided into sections, according to the age of the laying hens," he said. "And my prize rooster has a coop of his own."

He led the way. As the group drew near the long, low building, a terrific din came to their ears. Chickens were clucking wildly, and a rooster crowed shrilly.

"I wonder what's wrong?" Nan asked anxiously.

Before anyone could reply, one door of the henhouse burst open and Flossie, looking terrified, dashed out.

"Help! Help!" she cried out. "He's after me!"

CHAPTER IV

THE EGG HAT

AS Flossie ran down the hill toward her family, a huge brown rooster came after her, squawking loudly.

"Oh dear!" cried Mrs. Bobbsey.

Bert, in the lead, saw a small rock partly hidden by tall grass, lying directly in his sister's path.

"Watch out, Flossie!" he cried, but the warning came too late.

Flossie stumbled, and with a startled cry, fell down in a heap of arms and legs! The rooster was only a few feet behind!

"Pepper Pete, get away!" shouted Mr. Blaine.

The rooster stopped in its tracks. Bert and Nan rushed over to Flossie and helped her to stand.

"Are you hurt?" Mrs. Bobbsey asked anxiously, rushing up.

"No—I—I guess not!" Flossie answered.

"You are *so* hurt!" Freddie corrected, and pointed to a rough red mark on his twin's elbow.

Flossie tossed her blond curls and said bravely, "Oh—it's no worse than when my dolls get their paint scraped off."

Meanwhile, the farmer had captured his runaway rooster and now held it in his arms.

"Is his name really Pepper Pete?" Bert asked.

Sandy answered, "Yes, it is. He's Gramps' prize-winning rooster and king of the barnyard. He's really harmless but tries to act very important."

"I don't like him," said Flossie. "He tried to peck me."

"I'm sorry," Mr. Blaine said. "Perhaps you teased him."

"Not really," Flossie answered. "I just wouldn't let him have my circus hat."

"Circus hat?" the other children chorused.

Flossie explained that she had told Sandy about their plans for a home circus. The girl had gone to a trunk in the big barn and brought out a shiny green hat decorated with sequins for Flossie to wear.

"It belonged to my mother," Sandy said.

Flossie had put on the hat. When she bent down to look in a nest, it had fallen off.

"And when I started to pick it up, a chicken flew down from her perch and sat on it," Flossie continued. "I tried to shoo the chicken away, and then Pepper Pete came in from the next stall. That's when he tried to peck me. I got scared, and—"

"And Flossie flew the coop!" Bert joked, winking at the others.

Everyone laughed, then Mr. Blaine suggested that they all go into the hen house and get the hat. "Flossie, I guess you must have left the doors open between the coops."

"I'm sorry," the little girl said. "Is that bad?"

"Well, everything will be straightened out to-night," the farmer answered. "We'll call this visiting day for the hens. Tonight they'll go to their own perches, and then I'll close the doors between the coops."

"Why do the hens have to be separated?" Nan asked.

"Chickens of different ages often fight and that's not good for egg laying," Mr. Blaine replied. "Shall we go in now and find the circus hat?"

The Bobbseys stepped through the doorway. Before them were a series of coops separated by wire-mesh walls, each with a wire door. Every door stood open. Hundreds of hens were stalking about on the litter-covered floor. Many of them clucked at the visitors.

Flossie, still a little nervous, took Bert's hand. "I'll show you where my circus hat is," she said.

She took him to the coop next to Pepper Pete's. The stiff, green, spangled hat stood upside down on the floor under the front perch. As Bert reached in to get it, he laughed.

"Flossie, the chicken left you a present," he said. The little girl looked.

A large brown egg lay inside the hat!

"How bee-yoo-ti-ful!" cried Flossie in delight.

Mr. Blaine said that Pepper Pete probably had been afraid Flossie would disturb the hen while she was laying her egg. "That's why he chased you." Smiling, he added, "Flossie, take this egg home with you as a souvenir of your little adventure."

"Oh, thank you," the little girl said.

"Speaking of home," Mrs. Bobbsey said, consulting her watch, "we'd better be on our way, children."

Before the family left, Sandy gave each twin a short ride on Cockles. The small Shetland was very gentle and trotted slowly around the ring when Flossie and Freddie were on him.

The Bobbseys thanked the farm family and went to their car. Nan gave Sandy their address.

"Be sure to come see us when you're in Lakeport," she told the girl, and Sandy promised to do so.

A few minutes later the Bobbseys were back on the main highway leading to Lakeport.

"Sandy's a lot of fun," Nan said. "I hope we see her again sometime."

"I'm sure you will," her mother replied. "And her grandparents are fine people. They love Sandy dearly."

"But why didn't Mr. Blaine want us to talk about the Happy Top Circus?" Bert asked, perplexed.

His mother said she was not sure but guessed that Sandy's grandparents thought it might make her homesick and unhappy.

Nan nodded. "Circuses are fun to see, but I'd

rather live in one place than travel around the country all the time."

"Me, too," agreed Flossie, knowing how she would miss her home and chums in Lakeport.

Freddie grinned. "I'll bet Sandy doesn't mind it," he said, "and I wouldn't either! When I grow up I'm going to be a seal-trainer in the circus!"

At this moment the small boy looked out the car window and saw a dirt lane leading off the main highway. A sign beside it read Campers' Corner.

"Stop! Stop!" Freddie shouted, and Mrs. Bobbsey, thoroughly alarmed, applied the car brakes and pulled to the side of the road.

"What's the matter?" she exclaimed.

Her son pointed to the sign. "That's the camp we want to earn money for!"

"And I want to see it," Flossie added.

Mrs. Bobbsey was relieved that nothing was wrong and after warning Freddie that it was very dangerous to alarm a driver unnecessarily, she agreed to drive in and see the camp. She steered the car into the lane.

At the end of the dirt road a busy scene confronted the Bobbseys. Hammers pounded and saws buzzed as workmen constructed small log cabins for the young campers. The twins and their mother left the car for a closer inspection.

A husky workman pointed to spots where

other buildings would stand. The camp was planning to erect a mess hall, game room, crafts shop, and a small outdoor stage where the children could give plays.

"And over there," he said, motioning toward a half-cleared lot, "we'll have a baseball field."

"That's for me," Bert said.

"I'd like to come here myself," Freddie added.

"So would I," Nan and Flossie said in unison, looking at the clear blue water of Lake Metoka which could be seen beyond the clearing.

Reluctantly the Bobbseys left the pleasant spot and returned home. But now that they had seen it, the twins were filled with a fresh determination to earn money for Campers' Corner.

As the car rolled up the driveway of their house, the Bobbseys saw Dinah picking flowers in the back yard. She looked up and smiled.

"I'm glad to see you-all!" she said with a chuckle. She teased Freddie, "I thought maybe a bull had chased you and made you late."

"Freddie usually does get into some kind of trouble," Nan said.

Freddie made a face. "I never look for trouble. It just finds me! Anyway, this time it was Flossie who got chased."

The little girl showed the cook her circus hat and told of her adventure with Pepper Pete.

"And this is for your breakfast tomorrow, Dinah," she said, handing her the large brown egg. "It's country-fresh."

"Thank you. That's mighty nice."

Bert and Nan carried the vegetables and boxes of eggs into the kitchen. As Bert put his down on the kitchen table he glanced at a copy of the morning newspaper lying there. He looked at one of the headlines and suddenly stiffened. He could hardly believe what he read.

"Nan!" Bert cried. "Look at this!" He held up the news sheet, and read:

"HAPPY TOP CIRCUS SUFFERS
BAD FIRE IN MARYMONT!"

"Oh no!" his sister exclaimed.

By this time Mrs. Bobbsey and the younger twins had come into the kitchen. They too were startled by the news.

Nan read the whole story aloud. It said that the night before, the Happy Top Circus had given a performance in Marymont, a town fifty miles away. Sometime in the early morning hours a blaze had started, no one was sure how.

By the time the watchman discovered the fire in one of the smaller tents, it had spread to the main one. By the time the fire department put out the blaze, they had lost a good deal of equipment. Fortunately no one had been injured.

"I wonder if the circus will be able to show in Lakeport," said Mrs. Bobbsey. "They certainly can't give a performance without the main tent."

"Oh, it just *has* to come!" Freddie wailed, "no matter what!"

"Yes," Flossie added, "I want to see the circus Jack Horner Pie."

All during lunch, which the family ate on the screened side porch, the children talked of nothing but the circus fire. As they were finishing their lunch, the phone rang, and Mrs. Bobbsey went inside to answer it. At the same moment the twins heard sharp barks from the back yard. Bert and Freddie jumped up and hurried to the screen door leading to the yard.

"Howling coyotes!" cried Bert, dashing down the steps with Freddie and the girls behind.

Snoop was standing near the kitchen door with his back arched and his black fur standing straight up. Snap was barking and snarling furiously at a black-and-white terrier who was wolfing the food from Snap's and Snoop's dishes in quick, hungry gulps.

"Okay, okay!" Bert called. "Calm down, you fellows!"

Snap immediately ran up to his young master, but Snoop did not change his position.

"This is the same terrier that was in our kitchen," Nan said. Then she called, "Chips!

Come here, Chips!" Immediately the dog
trotted over to her. "He *is* Chips!" she cried
excitedly.

Flossie went up to the little animal and
stroked him.

"You poor doggie," she said. "Did you have a
nice place to stay last night?"

Just then a large navy-blue-and-white truck
turned into the Bobbseys' driveway and stopped.
The words DOG WARDEN were lettered on the
vehicle's sides.

The four children stared in surprise as a
heavy-set man wearing a white uniform jumped
from the driver's seat.

"Are you the Bobbseys?" the man shouted as
he brandished a long pole with a rope net attached to the end. Bert nodded.

"Then stand back!" the warden commanded.
"I've come for the dog!"

CHAPTER V

AN ELEPHANT'S SURPRISE

"WHICH dog?" Bert asked the warden. "And why do you want him?"

The warden pointed to the black-and-white terrier. "That little nuisance."

"Why are you after Chips? What has he done?" Nan wanted to know.

The warden did not reply. Instead, holding the large net, he edged closer to the terrier. All the time Chips was barking loudly and backing away.

Suddenly the dog-catcher made a swift lunge with his long pole, hoping to catch the dog unawares. But he miscalculated the distance and the net caught in a prickly shrub.

Bert took advantage of the opportunity to reason with the man. "I'm sure this terrier isn't dangerous," he said. "I think I know his owner. Won't you please tell us why you're after him?"

The warden frowned as he untangled his net.

"A boy down the street just told me a mad terrier tried to bite him and that the animal headed for the Bobbseys' back yard, so I rushed over here. I'll have to give this dog an examination to be sure he's all right."

With this the warden once more started after Chips. "Now come here, you!" he commanded.

The terrier squatted on his haunches, with one ear playfully cocked and his red tongue hanging out.

"Arf!" he barked, evidently thinking this was a game.

Chips waited until the long pole was almost touching him. Then he made a swift leap high into the air. With a swish of his tail, the dog back-flipped, landing on the grass. The next moment he was prancing about on his hind legs.

"He's doing a jig!" Flossie exclaimed, clapping her hands in glee.

Bang! the astonished dog-catcher dropped his pole on the concrete walk near the back steps.

The four twins howled with laughter at Chips' antics and the dog warden said, "What kind of an animal is this—he's very talented, I see!"

"He's a trick dog!" Flossie said, relieved that the grim look on the warden's face had changed to a good-natured expression.

Just then Mrs. Bobbsey came outside and glanced in amazement at the dog warden and

Chips. "What's going on here?" she asked.

"This is Chips and the warden's trying to take him away!" Flossie burst out.

Bert told the man about Mr. Riker and the terrier's first visit to the Bobbseys.

The warden listened intently. Finally he said, "I've had no report of a missing terrier from anyone named Riker. This animal seems to be all right, but just to be sure, I'd like to give him a quick check-up."

"Please do, officer," Mrs. Bobbsey said.

While the twins looked on anxiously, the dog warden examined the terrier's sturdy little body and peered into his throat. Finally he announced that he was sure Chips was 100 per cent healthy.

"Hurray! Hurray!" Freddie cheered.

"But," the warden went on, "I'll have to keep him at the pound until his owner turns up."

Mrs. Bobbsey, noticing the children's sad expressions, asked if her family might keep Chips until Mr. Riker put in a claim.

"Why of course," he replied. "If I should receive any inquiries about this terrier from his owner, I'll refer him to the Bobbseys."

"Thank you, sir," Bert said joyously.

The warden waved good-by and started to walk toward his truck. Nan and Bert hurried after him. The small twins followed.

"Who was the boy who reported Chips?" Nan asked.

"I don't know. Never saw him before."

"What did he look like?" Bert asked.

The man thought a moment, then said, "He was slightly taller than you and heavier. He wore blue jeans, a white shirt, and an orange baseball cap."

"Thanks," Bert said.

After the warden had driven off, Freddie spoke up. "Danny Rugg was wearing an orange baseball cap yesterday, Bert!"

"This sounds like one of Danny's mean tricks!" Nan said indignantly.

"But how does Danny know about Chips?" Flossie wondered.

"Easy," Freddie said promptly. "Danny's always spying on us—maybe he was hiding behind our garage when Chips was eating."

"He could have been," Bert agreed.

Mrs. Bobbsey had been listening to the conversation. Now she said, "Children, remember that you should never accuse anyone without having proof."

"I guess you're right, Mother," Freddie said.

Just then the sound of a car was heard turning into the driveway. A moment later Mr. Bobbsey's sedan drew to a stop in front of the garage. The twins' father, tall, slender, and muscular, got out.

"Hello, Mary!" He greeted his wife with a kiss and added, grinning, "What have our imps been up today?" He winked at the twins.

"Oh, Daddy, lots and lots of things happened!" Flossie exclaimed. "A big rooster chased me—and the dog warden's net got tangled up in the prickly bush, and we can keep Chips till Mr. Riker comes for him," she concluded breathlessly.

"Whoa! Start at the beginning!" her father begged laughingly. Chips bounded over and playfully began to sniff Mr. Bobbsey's shoe. Mr. Bobbsey patted the dog as the twins gave an excited account of the day's adventures.

"I'd say you've been very busy!" Mr. Bobbsey remarked when they finished. "Well, I suppose it will be all right to keep Chips until his owner claims him."

Freddie noticed a mysterious twinkle in his father's eyes. "Daddy, I smell a secret!" he cried happily. "What is it?"

"Yes, please tell us, Dick," said his wife.

Mr. Bobbsey grinned. "It's something for the children, and each of them is allowed one guess."

"Are we going on a vacation?" asked Nan.

"Is it something to eat?" Freddie wanted to know.

"Or to play with?" Flossie put in.

"I'll bet it's something connected with the circus," Bert deduced.

Mr. Bobbsey hesitated and Nan pleaded, "Won't you give us a little hint?"

"Bert and Flossie are closest!" Mr. Bobbsey announced. "I had lunch today with Jim Allen, who has a canvas factory here in town. I placed an order with him for a back-yard tent."

"Oh, boy!" Freddie shouted and immediately turned a somersault.

Flossie gave her father a big hug and cried, "You're a Santa Claus Daddy!"

The older twins were also thrilled and wanted to know when the tent would arrive. Mr. Bobbsey said it would be delivered the next morning.

The four children could hardly wait and were up bright and early the following day. Flossie and Freddie kept busy during the morning hours playing with Chips, who had slept overnight in Snap's enclosed pen. The two dogs had become good friends.

Nan and Bert, meanwhile, phoned the warden to see if anyone had inquired about Chips. But no one had reported a missing terrier, and the lost-and-found column in the Lakeport newspaper had no advertisement for such a pet.

The older twins returned home and sat down on the grass in the back yard to watch their brother and sister play with Snap and Chips. Chuckling, Nan said, "You know, Bert, 'Egg-

Beater' would be a better name for Chips, too. Or 'Waggo,' for his tail!"

All the twins agreed Waggo was a perfect name, and Freddie suggested, "Let's call him Waggo while he's here."

Laughingly Nan called the black-and-white terrier to her side. "Chips," she said, trying to make her voice very solemn, "we hereby re-name you Waggo."

The frisky little animal barked three times and walked around on his hind legs.

"I think Waggo likes his new name," Flossie said.

By the middle of the afternoon the tent had not arrived and Bert decided to call Mr. Allen and check the order. Nan, Flossie, and Freddie waited nearby while he dialed the manufacturer's number.

After a few minutes of conversation, Bert said, "Thanks, Mr. Allen. That's good news, and of course we don't mind waiting for our tent!"

Bert replaced the phone in its cradle and said to the other children, "Our tent will be delivered later in the week because Mr. Allen's factory has a big, special rush order to get out. All other deliveries have to be held up."

"But—but—" sputtered Freddie in disappointment.

His brother smiled. "The big order," he continued, "is to make new canvas to replace the burned tents of the Happy Top Circus!"

"You mean the circus may still come to Lakeport!" squealed Flossie, and Bert nodded.

"Wonderful!" cried Nan, and the little twins hugged each other, agreeing they did not mind waiting for their own tent.

That night at dinner Mr. Bobbsey announced that the Happy Top Circus would definitely arrive in town the next evening, only one day late. Performances were scheduled for three days following.

"Goody!" exclaimed Flossie, and everyone broke into pleased smiles.

"Any news on Chips' owner?" asked Mr. Bobbsey.

Nan and Bert shook their heads, telling of the inquiries they had made that day. "And Chips has a new name," Nan told her father. "We're going to call him 'Waggo.'"

"I hope you children are giving Snap lots of attention," said Mrs. Bobbsey with a smile.

"We'll always love Snap!" Flossie declared.

The boys decided that Waggo should have a doghouse of his own, so early the next day they went to the lumberyard for boards. Then they started work in back of their house. Nan and Flossie busied themselves making a separate run for the terrier in Snap's large enclosure. This work took most of the day and the twins were glad to go to bed early, eager to visit the circus grounds first thing in the morning.

After breakfast the next day, the four children started off together. As they walked toward downtown Lakeport, Freddie kept singing over and over:

"The circus is here!
Let's give a big cheer!"

"It's the best time of year!" Flossie added.

When they reached the circus area the twins saw a scene of bustling activity. Equipment was being unloaded from the trucks, men were digging foundations to support the tent poles, and many sightseers were wandering over the grounds.

Nan pointed out some souvenir and refreshment stands that had been set up already.

"I love circus food," said Freddie. "I wish they were selling hot dogs and ice cream now."

Bert grinned. "Right after breakfast?"

Bert saw his friend Charlie Mason. Charlie was also twelve years old. The good-looking, dark-haired boy was heading for a large tent already set up. The sign over it read MENAGERIE.

"Hey, Charlie!" Bert called.

His friend turned around and waved to the twins. "Hi! I'm going to get a job carrying water for the elephants! Want to come?"

"Let's" Freddie urged. "We can make money for Campers' Corner."

"Okay," Bert agreed.

The girls preferred to walk around the grounds. Perhaps they would see some of the circus performers. "We'll meet you outside the menagerie tent in an hour," Nan told Bert.

The three boys went inside the tent. The boys explained their errand to a workman and asked whom they should see.

"Speak to the head elephant-trainer," said the workman, pointing out a man of medium height with gray hair. "His name is Amos."

The boys found Amos, who listened impatiently to the job request. "I jes' hired a couple o' fellows," he said, motioning behind him. The trainer strode off.

"Too bad," said Charlie, shrugging and turning to see who the boys were. Danny Rugg and his friend Jack Westley! Jack, also a bully, often helped Danny play tricks.

Danny caught sight of Charlie and the Bobbseys. "Yah! Yah!" he jeered, swaggering up to them. "The early bird gets the worm." While saying this, the bully set a pail of water on the sawdust-covered floor behind him.

About to retort, Bert noticed that a large elephant standing behind Danny had stretched out his trunk and was drinking from the pail. The elephant wore a velvet mantle with the name DOLLY embroidered on it.

"She's thirsty!" thought Bert. But instead of swallowing the water, Dolly straightened her trunk and shot the water out in a great stream. It splashed squarely across Danny Rugg's white sport shirt!

"Hey!" cried the bully, whirling around.

Beside himself with rage, Danny picked up the half-emptied pail. Before anyone could stop him, he hurled the heavy metal container at the large beast.

"That'll fix you!" Danny cried.

CHAPTER VI

BERT TO THE RESCUE

SOME distance from the menagerie, Nan and Flossie were strolling around looking for performers. They had met several of their school friends excitedly darting to and fro.

"But we haven't seen one real circus person!" Flossie sighed.

"I guess they're all busy practicing their acts for the performance," Nan replied. "Or maybe they're home."

"Nan," Flossie asked, "where do the circus people live?"

The older girl looked around the area. "I think they live in trailers," she replied. "Maybe they're camped beyond those trees, near the lake." Nan pointed to a thick grove of trees bordering the park.

"Trailers!" Flossie exclaimed. "You mean the houses on wheels?"

As Flossie said this, a friendly voice behind

the two sisters sang out, "That's kee-rect!"

The sisters turned and saw a short, chubby man smiling at them. He was wearing a black-and-white striped suit, bright pink shirt, and a brown derby hat.

"Excuse me for eavesdropping," the gaily dressed man apologized, "but as I was walking by I heard you girls say you wanted to meet some circus people." He extended his hand. "I'm K. T. Duncan, owner of the Happy Top Circus."

Nan and Flossie were delighted. "How do you do," they said in unison and introduced themselves. The circus owner pumped their hands heartily.

Flossie hesitated, then asked, "Is—is your name really *Katie?* I thought that was a girl's name."

Nan tried not to smile at Flossie's mistake, but K. T. Duncan gave a jolly laugh. He explained that his real name was Kenneth Thomas Duncan.

"But everyone calls me K. T.—first two initials," he said. "And you girls can, too."

"Thank you, K. T.," Nan said, already feeling at ease with this jovial man.

"You can call me F. B., for Flossie Bobbsey!" her little sister said gravely.

The circus owner's gray eyes twinkled in amusement. Then he waved to a boy and a girl who were walking toward him. "These are my children," he explained.

"Hi, Dad!" said the girl, who was pretty and dark-haired with blue eyes and a heart-shaped face. She looked about eight years old.

"This is my daughter, Jandy," said K. T., "and this is Jimmy," he added. The Bobbseys smiled at the ten-year-old boy who looked very much like his father in build and features.

K. T. introduced Nan and Flossie.

"Welcome to our circus," Jandy said, and her brother added, "We hope you enjoy seeing it."

"Oh, we will!" Flossie assured them. "We can't wait until tomorrow. Please tell us what's in the Jack Horner Pie!"

K. T. chuckled. "That's a secret I can't let out of the cracker box!"

"We're all curious about it," Nan said, and mentioned that she and Flossie each had a twin brother.

"Where are they?" Jimmy asked eagerly.

Flossie explained that the boys had gone to the menagerie tent hoping to find water-carrying jobs.

"Let's walk over there now," Jandy suggested.

On the way to the animal quarters Nan asked the Duncan children whether they performed in the circus. Jandy said they were acrobats.

"I just know you're good ones!" Flossie remarked.

"Some day we hope to be," Jimmy replied modestly.

Smiling at his children fondly, K. T. said he thought they were top notch already. "But you can judge for yourselves at the show," he told Nan and Flossie.

"When is the new main tent going to be put up?" Nan asked the circus owner as they drew near the menagerie entrance. "My brother Bert said Mr. Allen was making it for you."

"That's right. I've known Jim Allen for years," K. T. explained. "His factory makes all our tents. He said our order would be delivered late this afternoon."

Flossie in turn told the Duncans about the back-yard tent Mr. Bobbsey had ordered for their own little circus.

"You'll have lots of fun giving it," Jandy said with keen interest.

Just then a loud shriek of horror pierced the air. Everyone stopped short, exchanging startled glances.

"Dad! That came from the menagerie tent!" Jimmy exclaimed. "It sounded like a boy."

His father nodded and raced toward the tent. The four children followed him. Nan's heart was thumping. Bert, Freddie, and Charlie were in the tent. Had something happened to them?

Once inside the quarters, they noticed that a sizable crowd had gathered at the far end. At the same moment they saw a gigantic elephant clutching a boy in its trunk and swinging him around in the air.

As Nan, Flossie, and Jandy hurried closer, the boy gave a terrified yell and kicked his legs wildly in an effort to free himself.

"That's Danny Rugg!" Nan gasped.

Flossie's eyes were wide with fear. While she did not like Danny, she did not want him to get hurt.

K. T. Duncan was pushing through the crowd, giving orders to several helpers who were behind him. Jandy pointed to two boys running toward the elephant from another direction.

"I wonder what they're going to do," she said to Nan and Flossie.

"Why, they're Bert and Freddie, our twins!" Flossie exclaimed, and Nan looked worried.

Bert was carrying a small paper bag. Nan watched in alarm as her brother approached the elephant. Bert reached into the bag and held his palm out toward the huge beast.

There was a sudden hush in the large tent when Bert said in a loud clear voice, "Please put him down, Dolly. Come on, girl—"

The circus animal stared at Bert's hand for a moment. Then, with a loud bellow, Dolly stamped her right front hoof and lowered Danny Rugg. The bully's face was white as paste when his feet touched the floor.

"Bravo! Bravo!" cheered a spectator.

Nan rushed over to her twin. "Oh Bert, you were wonderful!" she exclaimed. "How did you ever make Dolly obey?"

Bert grinned and showed Nan what he had

offered the elephant for Danny's release. Peanuts! "It was Freddie's idea to get these for Dolly," he explained.

The elephant, now calm, nuzzled Bert's hand with her wrinkled trunk and took the few remaining nuts. Nan turned around to see where Danny Rugg had gone. The bully was talking loudly to K. T. Duncan, who had made certain the boy had suffered no injuries.

"That old elephant was going to throw me out of the tent," Danny was saying angrily. "Didn't she try to, Jack?" he asked his buddy, who stood beside him.

"She sure did," Jack replied quickly.

A puzzled expression came over K. T. Duncan's face. "How did the accident happen?" he asked, as the Bobbseys, Charlie, and the Duncan children came up.

With a side glance at Jack, Danny said that he had been standing in front of the elephant when the animal had reached out for him and picked him up.

"But—but—" Freddie began. At a look from Bert, the small boy stopped speaking.

"That doesn't sound like Dolly," Jimmy Duncan spoke up. "She's the gentlest elephant we own."

The onlookers began to leave, and K. T. Duncan walked over to Bert. "Thanks for saving the day. I guess you're Bert, Nan's twin." The man turned to Freddie. "And you must be Freddie, who thought of the peanuts."

The Bobbsey boys shook hands with the circus owner, then Nan introduced Charlie to the Duncans. K. T.'s usually jolly face was serious as he said, "Without the help of you Bobbsey lads, this accident could have become serious."

Jimmy spoke up. "Dad, where's Amos? He's supposed to make sure no children get too close to the animals."

At these words the head elephant-trainer entered the tent and sauntered over to K. T. Amos said he had just heard of the accident.

"These two boys said they'd look after Dolly while I went for somethin' to eat." The trainer pointed accusingly to Danny and Jack.

Danny nudged his friend slyly. Jack cleared his throat and said haltingly, "I don't—er—want to be a squealer but—well—Bert Bobbsey threw a stick at Dolly. She thought Danny did it—"

"Oh!" Nan gasped and Bert flushed angrily.

Charlie Mason could keep silent no longer. "That's not true!" he cried out. "I'm not going to let Bert be accused of something he didn't do!"

Charlie told about Dolly squirting water at Danny Rugg and how the boy had thrown the pail at the elephant. The beast had stepped aside in time to duck the pail, which had crashed against a wooden tent support.

"I can guess the rest," K. T. put in. "Elephants never forget, and Dolly decided to teach Danny a lesson. Is that right, Danny?"

The circus-owner looked around, but there was no reply. Danny Rugg and Jack Westley had sneaked out of the tent while Charlie was talking. K. T. said that since no harm had been done it would be best to forget the incident. He warned Amos, however, not to let Danny or Jack come near the elephants again.

"How did Dolly get her name?" Flossie asked as she glanced up at the peaceful-looking elephant.

Jandy explained that the elephant had been born in the African jungle where most circus elephants come from. She became very restless when she was captured and brought to the United States.

"What a hard time the trainers had trying to ride her," Jimmy interrupted. "She would bellow and stamp whenever anyone came near her."

"How was the elephant finally trained?" Nan asked.

Jandy went on to say that one trainer finally decided to use a heavy, life-size doll instead of a real person in teaching the elephant to carry weight on her back. The elephant soon grew fond of the doll-rider strapped to her back and would parade proudly around the circus arena.

"She got to like all dolls so much," Jandy concluded with a laugh, "I gave her the name Dolly."

The other children laughed and Flossie said, "I love dolls, too! Dolly and I will be good friends."

K. T. smiled at the little girl and reached into his coat pocket. He brought out five passes for the circus performance the next day.

"My treat for the Bobbsey twins and Charlie," he said, giving them each one ticket. "I hope you enjoy the show."

"Oh thank you! Thank you!" chorused the five children.

Jandy, smiling at her new friends, whispered something in her father's ear. He nodded, consulted his wrist watch, and announced that he must get back to work.

"So long, children. Have fun."

After he had left, Jandy said, "Daddy told me I could invite all of you to have lunch with us today in our cookhouse! I hope you can."

"How nice!" Nan remarked, and Flossie asked what the cookhouse was.

"The large tent where we have our circus dining room and kitchen," Jandy replied.

"Oh boy!" Freddie exclaimed. "Will we have a Jack Horner Pie?"

Jimmy Duncan laughed. "No, but it'll be a good lunch anyway."

The Bobbseys and Charlie were happy to accept the Duncans' invitation. The older boys said they would call home to ask permission from Mrs. Bobbsey and Mrs. Mason.

"You can use the phone in Dad's office." Jandy pointed out a trailer located near the main gate.

As Bert and Charlie walked toward the trailer, they heard Flossie call, "I'm coming too!" Catching up to them, she said she wanted to see what an office on wheels looked like.

When the three reached the trailer, which was unoccupied, Charlie stepped inside. As Bert waited to help Flossie, she suddenly shrieked.

"What's the matter?" he asked, as she started to tremble.

Flossie stared beyond Bert and pointed toward the street. Finally she gasped out:

"There's—there's a giant as high as the sky over there!"

CHAPTER VII

A COOKHOUSE LUNCH

"A GIANT!" echoed Bert in disbelief. "Where?"

"He's . . . he's walking up and down the street . . . right outside the circus gate," Flossie insisted. "Must be a Jack-in-the-Beanstalk giant, Bert!"

Her brother grinned and Charlie, who had overheard Flossie, stepped out of the office trailer to take a look.

"Show us your giant, Flossie," Charlie said curiously.

Flossie pointed. Sure enough, when the boys turned to look, they saw an extremely tall man standing near the main gate. Bert estimated the man's height at about twelve feet. He was wearing a red-plaid suit and bright-yellow straw hat.

"See, he *is* a giant!" Flossie said.

By now the man had noticed the three children staring at him. With tremendous steps he lifted one leg, then the other, over the main gate and strode toward them.

Suddenly Bert and Charlie exclaimed together, "He's walking on stilts!" Both boys chuckled at the half-puzzled, half-relieved look on Flossie's face.

"You mean," the little girl said, "he's only a pretend giant?"

"That's right," Charlie stated.

As the man on stilts strutted toward the children he gave a broad smile.

"Hello, Goldilocks!" he greeted Flossie. "How's the weather down there?"

"It's fine, Daddy Longlegs," Flossie giggled.

The man laughed heartily when Bert explained that his sister had mistaken him for a giant. "Ho Ho! That's good." The stilt-walker winked at Flossie. "I'm a stunt man for the Happy Top Circus. They call me Stretch.

"Right now," he went on, "I'm practicing my special walk. Soon I'll stroll around Lakeport carrying a circus poster telling of the opening performance. Then tomorrow morning I'll be in the parade with the clowns."

Flossie was fascinated. "Walking on stilts must be lots of fun. I wish I could try it."

"It's much safer for most people to walk on their own two feet," said the stunt man with a grin.

The children laughed, and the "giant" took his leave to continue practicing.

Bert and Charlie telephoned their mothers and received permission for the children to have lunch with the Duncans. Flossie and the boys hurried back to join the others.

"The cookhouse tent is back near the trailer colony," Jandy said, leading the way.

"Jandy and Jimmy live in a trailer," Freddie told his twin as the group walked along. "They're going to show it to us after lunch."

When they reached the trailer section near the lake, it appeared to be deserted. Jandy said this was because everyone was eating lunch.

"Wow! There must be a *zillion* trailers," Freddie exclaimed, glancing about at the rows and rows of mobile homes.

Jimmy smiled. "I think we have about two hundred altogether, besides some small sleeping tents."

"Here's the cookhouse!" Jandy said, indicating a large tent which the Bobbseys had not seen from the main part of the circus grounds.

"Boy! Something sure smells good!" Freddie sniffed the air.

The children walked inside the tent and the visitors saw that it was crowded with circus people. Some were in costume while others wore regular summer clothes.

Jimmy led the way among the long dining

tables and stopped at one in the center. Only one person was seated at it—a slim, attractive woman.

"This is our mother!" Jandy told her new friends, introducing the twins and Charlie.

Mrs. Duncan smiled and her dark eyes lighted up. "I'm so happy to meet you all," she said in a low, musical voice. "Everyone calls me Carla, and I'd like you to, also."

"It's nice to meet you—Carla," Nan said, and they all shook hands with the woman.

As the children took seats across the table from one another, Freddie turned to Carla and asked, "Are you in the Happy Top Circus too?"

Jimmy Duncan said proudly, "Mom's our very best acrobat!"

Just then a smiling waiter approached the table carrying a large tray laden with food. He placed dishes of steaming beef stew before Carla and the children. A green salad, hot crisp rolls, and milk followed.

"Ummmm, this looks good!" Flossie said.

Freddie, however, was staring at his meal in astonishment. "I thought circus people ate only circus food," he said, picking up his fork.

Jimmy's eyes twinkled. "Like peanuts, popcorn, and crackerjacks?" he joked.

The small boy looked serious. "Why yes," he replied, adding, "we have beef stew at home, too."

As Freddie picked up his fork, four Happy Top entertainers came to the table and took seats near the Duncans and their visitors. Jimmy and Jandy introduced the newcomers.

One was Lank, the circus thin man, and his companion, Daisy Dimples, who was the fattest woman the twins had ever seen. As she sat down on two chairs provided by the waiter,

Daisy declared she weighed four hundred pounds.

"And this is Teeny," Jandy put in, indicating a jolly-looking midget man who was no taller than Freddie.

"And here's Gee-Gee!" she added.

The twins knew instantly that Gee-Gee was a circus clown. His green eyes were ringed with black make-up, his face smeared with blobs of grease paint, and he wore a shaggy brown wig.

The Bobbseys were thrilled at meeting the side-show members and a true-to-life clown. Freddie was so intrigued he forgot to eat his lunch!

Daisy Dimples gave him a big wink. "Little fellow," she said teasingly, "if you don't want your stew, I'll take it. I'm so hungry I could devour an elephant!"

Freddie laughed, and assured Daisy he was certainly going to eat his lunch! When the waiter brought the circus people their meal, Lank frowned.

"This stew is too fattening for me," he declared.

Hailing the waiter, the thin man asked for a lettuce-and-carrot salad. "If I gain weight," he joked, "I'll be out of a job. No circus wants a fat thin man!"

"How do you children like our circus?" Gee-Gee the clown asked the visitors.

"The Happy Top is *tops!*" Bert exclaimed. "We can hardly wait to see you all in the show."

Suddenly, as the others chattered, Nan remembered Sandy Blaine, and told the Happy Top people about the circus girl. "You should see Sandy ride bareback!" she added.

Clatter! Gee-Gee dropped his fork on the table, and Bert noticed that the clown had a peculiar expression in his lively green eyes.

"Excuse me," Gee-Gee apologized. "Tell us more about Sandy."

Nan went on to explain why Sandy was not allowed to visit the circus. Carla looked sympathetic, saying she hoped the little girl would be reunited with her parents before too long.

"I hope it will be soon, too," Gee-Gee said in a low voice.

After a moment of silence, Freddie spoke up. "We have a dog at home that can do swell tricks." He described Waggo. "He's good enough to be in the circus."

Teeny, the midget, grinned widely. "I don't know about Waggo, but we could ask K. T. about an act featuring the Bobbsey twins," he said.

"Could you?" Flossie and Freddie cried together excitedly.

"Sure." Lank nodded approvingly. "Two sets of twins who look so much alike would be a great novelty!"

The fat lady laughed. "You could sit on the platform next to me." To the small twins she added, "Can you sing or dance, or do you have double joints like our Rubber Man?"

Flossie looked doubtful. "We all have rubbers at home, but I don't know about our joints," she said, giggling.

At the same moment Freddie's attention was attracted by a short, black-haired man walking toward the tent entrance. He wore a dark mustache which looked as though it were painted on.

"Who is that man, Jimmy?" Freddie asked.

The Duncan boy explained it was the dog-trainer, Mr. Rett. Jimmy snapped his fingers. "If your Waggo does tricks," he said, "you should see Mr. Rett. One of his dogs is sick. Waggo might be a good substitute."

The small twins exchanged glances. This idea sounded exciting. Perhaps Waggo's owner would not mind his pet being in a circus for one performance. After a dessert of ice cream and cookies, the Bobbseys and Charlie bade Carla and their other grown-up friends good-by, then followed Jimmy and Jandy to the dog-trainer's tent.

They entered and saw a miniature-sized ring at one end. There were several cages filled with dogs of various sizes and breeds around the tent. The animals barked as the children walked up to Mr. Rett.

Before Jimmy had a chance to make introductions, the trainer said gruffly, "I'm too busy now to see anyone."

Nan and Flossie were taken back by the man's brusqueness, but Jandy quickly explained the purpose of their visit. The dog-trainer's attitude changed in a twinkling. In a friendlier tone he said:

"That's different!" He gave the twins a searching stare. "So you have a clever trick dog, eh?"

"Oh yes," Flossie bubbled. "He can—" She broke off, for Bert had given his sister a warning look. Somehow he did not like the dog-trainer. A greedy expression had come into the man's eyes at mention of Waggo. Bert had a feeling that the terrier would not be happy with Mr. Rett, even for a short time.

"I'd like to see your mutt. If he's any good, I'll buy him!" the man said.

Nan shook her head hastily. She too did not like Mr. Rett. "I guess we'd better keep Waggo," she told the man, "in case his rightful owner does find out we have him."

At this, Mr. Rett became angry. In a curt voice he said, "Then why did you come here? Maybe you'll change your mind." He scowled at the twins and turned his back.

The children left the tent. Charlie said he didn't care for the man, and Jimmy admitted that the trainer was not popular among the other performers.

Before the Lakeport visitors left to go home, the circus brother and sister took them through their neat, cozy home-trailer. It contained a living-dining room, a shiny kitchen, two bedrooms, and a bath.

"It's almost like a doll house!" cried Flossie, delighted. "But big enough for real people."

Jimmy and Jandy smiled as they walked with their new friends to the circus gate. "We have fun living in it," said Jandy. "But sometimes we'd like to live in one town where we could make friends with people like all of you!"

"I hope you can sometime," said Nan.

The twins and Charlie thanked the two Duncan children for all they had done and said they would see them again soon.

When the Bobbseys reached home they found Dinah baking brownies. She gave the twins several of the tasty little cakes, then listened in amazement to their morning's experience.

Then Bert asked Nan, "Did Gee-Gee remind you of somebody?"

Nan laughed. "Not with all his clown make-up on. Why?"

Bert shrugged. "Maybe I just imagined it."

Flossie was looking anxiously out the window. "I hope," she said, "it'll stay nice for the circus tomorrow."

"It better not rain!" Freddie stated.

Dinah spoke up. "I'm sure it won't, honey lambs. But I'll tune in the radio weather report. It's 'bout time for one."

The cook switched on the kitchen radio and dialed to the Lakeport station. In a moment the announcer's voice was heard saying:

"Tomorrow's weather: Fair and warm—" The man suddenly broke off. "Just a moment, folks. Here's a special bulletin."

The twins and Dinah listened curiously. The next second they were stunned to hear the announcer exclaim excitedly:

"Flash—Lakeport residents. Call everyone inside immediately! A ferocious lion has just escaped from the Happy Top Circus!"

CHAPTER VIII

LIONS!

THE news that a lion had escaped from the Happy Top Circus frightened everyone in the Bobbsey kitchen. For a moment there was silence, then Nan spoke.

"I hope the lion will be caught before anyone gets hurt," she said with a shudder.

Flossie looked out the window and said fearfully, "Me, too. I'm glad *we're* home."

"Now don't worry, children," Dinah said, trying to keep her voice calm. But her eyes had grown very wide. This always happened when she was upset.

"That lion won't get you while I'm around!" Freddie assured his sisters in a bold voice.

Bert held up his hand for silence. The radio announcer was giving more details of the incident. Dinah and the children leaned forward to catch every word.

The announcer reported that trucks carrying

the wild animals to the circus had arrived in Lakeport an hour earlier. The vehicles had been delayed en route because of needed repairs.

It was while the beasts were being transferred from the trucks to cages in the menagerie tent that the lion had made his dash for freedom. The animal had raced through the tent and across the grounds out of sight. He was thought to be hiding in the vicinity of the circus grounds.

"Stay inside your homes and keep tuned for further details," the announcer concluded.

At that moment a car stopped in the Bobbseys' driveway and Sam Johnson, Dinah's husband, got out. Walking as though he did not have a care in the world, he ambled into the kitchen.

"My gracious, Sam Johnson!" his wife scolded. "You better not be roamin' around with that dangerous lion loose."

Sam, who was lean and wiry, grinned widely. "No lion would want to eat me," he replied, chuckling. "I'm too tough. Besides, I 'magine the beast will be caught before long."

Nan looked worried. "I hope Mother and Dad have heard the report and stay inside."

"I'm sure they're safe," Bert assured his sister. "Dad's at the office and Mother's helping at the church bazaar."

Suddenly Freddie let out a startled, "Oh!" and yelled that Waggo, Snap, and Snoop were outdoors. The two boys dashed out the kitchen door and ran to the enclosure behind the garage. A few minutes later they returned with the dogs.

"Where's Snoop?" Flossie asked.

Bert said they could not find the cat anywhere.

"Oh dear." Flossie's eyes filled with tears. "I'm 'fraid the lion will catch Snoop and gobble him up!"

Sam leaned down and patted the little girl's shoulder. "That could never happen," he said kindly. "A lion is really only a big cat. And not even a big wild cat would hurt another cat."

As Flossie dried her tears, Sam said, "Well, I have to get goin'," and walked toward the kitchen door.

"Mercy!" Dinah gasped. "Where?"

Her husband explained he had just picked up Mr. Bobbsey's automobile which had been at a local garage for minor repairs. He had promised to drive to the lumberyard for the twins' father and on the way back stop for Mrs. Bobbsey at the church.

"Please don't leave now!" Dinah begged. "Lions are mighty strong—this one might jump through the car windshield."

Though Bert doubted this would happen, he agreed that Sam should wait a while. Nan said she would call the church and also the lumberyard and explain to her parents.

At that moment the telephone rang. Nan hurried to answer it. The call was from Mrs. Bobb-

sey who had heard about the escaped lion. To
her daughter's surprise and relief she reported
that the beast had just been captured by police
officers behind the menagerie tent. Nan returned
to the kitchen and told the others.

"Praise be!" declared Dinah.

"How did Mother find out?" Freddie wanted
to know. "We haven't heard it on the radio yet."

Nan said that Mrs. Bobbsey was still at the
church bazaar. A policeman had come to the
church a short while before to tell everyone
there of the lion's capture.

Dinah heaved a grateful sigh. "Now I can
start supper with a peaceful mind." She turned
to her chore, humming a gay tune.

"Let's look for Snoop," Flossie urged Nan,
and the girls went outside to search for the pet.

Bert suggested that he and Freddie go with
Sam to Mr. Bobbsey's lumberyard. The good-
natured man said he would be pleased to have
company.

"You boys ready?" Sam asked.

"I am," Bert said, looking around for his
brother. Freddie was nowhere in sight.

"He went to the basement," Dinah spoke up.
Bert called down from the head of the steps,
"Freddie! Hurry up!"

"Coming!" the small boy answered.

Bert and Sam went outside and stepped into
the car just as Freddie arrived. He was carrying

a crabbing net and a long piece of clothesline.

"What are those for?" Bert asked curiously as Freddie took a seat beside him.

"In case the lion escapes again," Freddie replied staunchly. "I can catch him with this net —it's like the dog warden's—and tie him to a tree with the clothesline."

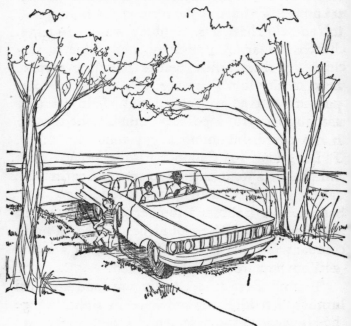

Bert and Sam laughed, and Sam said it was always wise to be prepared. He backed the car out of the driveway and soon they were on their way toward Lake Metoka. Freddie started to sing:

"Hi, ho, hi, ho—
Off to the lumberyard we go—"

Though Mr. Bobbsey's business property was only a short distance from the Bobbsey home and could have been reached in a few minutes, Bert asked Sam please to drive them the long way around. The route he requested would take them along the outskirts of Lakeport, and the twins loved to ride through the countryside.

"Sure," Sam said affably.

He made a right-hand turn and for several minutes the car went through the residential part of town. An archway of tall trees provided a cool, shaded drive. Then Sam came to a main highway. He drove along this for two miles. Finally he turned into a long, narrow lane which led to the rear of the lumberyard and the lake.

Suddenly Freddie cried out, "Bert and Sam —there's a lion back of us!"

Screech! Sam applied the brakes in a hurry and the car stopped short.

"Where?" cried Bert, as he and Sam looked around. All they saw was the shiny green foliage bordering the twisting road ahead.

"I don't see any animal," Sam said. "Not even a squirrel."

Both Sam and Bert glanced at Freddie. The small boy was laughing. "I fooled you. The big cat was captured, remember?"

"Whew!" Sam wiped his brow and started the car again. "Better not try that again, Freddie. I might've driven right up a tree."

"That's right," Bert told his brother, sternly.

As they drove along, the boys told Sam about their morning and lunch at the Happy Top Circus. In turn, Sam said that he had always loved the circus and even had run away to join a small traveling one when he was a boy. But he had changed his mind and returned home two hours later when he became hungry.

Presently Bert noticed that his brother had become unusually quiet. Freddie was kneeling on the car seat and looking out the rear window. The next moment he cried out:

"Sam! Bert! Look at the big cat!"

"Oh no, you're not foolin' me again with another lion story," declared Sam and kept on driving.

"No, Freddie—" Bert started to say sternly.

"Please, Bert," the little boy insisted. "See what's here."

Bert finally turned around. "Snoop!" he cried out in surprise. Hearing this, Sam pulled to the side of the road.

"Sure 'nough," he declared, looking over his shoulder. The Bobbsey cat was curled, half-hidden, under a folded blanket on the back seat. Now he blinked sleepily at the trio.

"Well, at least Freddie *did* see a big cat this

time." Bert chuckled. "But I'm glad it's Snoop instead of a lion." Freddie grinned.

As the car turned a bend in the road, the boys saw their father's lumberyard ahead. Beyond, the waters of Lake Metoka sparkled in the sunlight.

Then Freddie saw something that made him gasp and sit bold upright. He rubbed his eyes in disbelief. Wordlessly he nudged Bert and pointed out the window. The older boy took one look, then cried out in astonishment:

"Sam," he said. "This is no joke. There are *three* lions—right ahead of us!"

CHAPTER IX

SHADOWY FIGURES

AT Bert's startling words, Sam stopped the car abruptly.

"Three lions!" he echoed.

Hopping up and down with excitement as he clutched his crabbing net, Freddie cried, "Over there!"

Huddled together on the side of the dirt lane, Sam saw three tawny cubs. "Baby lions!" he gasped.

Bert rolled up the car windows so Snoop could not leap out, then Sam and the twins cautiously approached the cubs. Freddie leaned over, about to pat one of the small animals. "Grr-rr-rr!" snarled the cub, its short hair bristling.

Freddie retreated hastily. "They're not very friendly, even if they are babies," he remarked.

"Better stay back," Sam advised the boys.

Just then Bert noticed that the cub which

Freddie had tried to pat had a thorn in his right front paw and pointed this out to the others.

Immediately sympathetic, Freddie said, "If we could only pull the thorn out, he'd feel better."

Sam removed a clean handkerchief from his pants' pocket. "I'll see what I can do," he offered.

Bending down, Sam grasped the wounded cub firmly with one hand. With the other, he placed the handkerchief over the thorn and gently pulled it out. Surprisingly, as if he knew he was being helped, the young lion had not uttered a sound.

"You're a swell animal doctor," Freddie praised Sam.

"What'll we do with these cubs?" Bert asked. "We can't leave 'em here."

Freddie's face lighted up. "We can take them home," he suggested. "I'll bet we could teach the cubs to be pets."

His brother chuckled. "Don't forget they'll be grown-up lions someday, Freddie."

The small boy was not discouraged. "Then we'll sell them to a circus."

Bert said he was sure the cubs already belonged to the Happy Top Circus, and had run away.

"Must be," Sam agreed.

The three discussed what they should do. It was finally decided that Sam would go for Mr. Bobbsey while the boys remained to guard the baby lions. Sam drove off.

Bert and Freddie sat down on the grass. They watched the cubs playfully chase one another in circles.

Soon Sam returned with Mr. Bobbsey. The boys' father left the car and hurried over to see the animals. He shook his head in amazement. "They're the most unusual visitors I've ever had near the lumberyard," he declared.

Bert laughed, then told of his idea that the cubs belonged to the Happy Top Circus.

"I'm sure you're right," Mr. Bobbsey said. "Let's take them to the circus grounds and find out."

They placed the animals in a deep wooden crate Sam had brought along. Then they fastened a light net cover to the top to prevent the lions' escape. Freddie and Bert climbed into the rear of the car and handed Snoop to their father. Then Sam put the crate on the seat between the boys.

Snoop instantly began meowing and sniffing curiously at the wooden box. Freddie grinned at their pet's excitement and said, "Snoop's saying hello to his jungle cousins."

The car started off and soon arrived at the circus grounds. Near the gate, Mr. Bobbsey noticed his friend Jim Allen and pointed him out. He was a tall, lanky man.

"Mr. Allen's talking to K. T.," observed Bert, who had told his father about the Duncan family.

Mr. Bobbsey, Freddie, and Bert left the car and Sam remained with the animals. Mr. Allen and K. T. had already seen them and were hurrying through the gate.

Introductions were made, then Bert asked about the lion cubs, telling how they had been found.

K. T.'s eyebrows raised in amazement. "I'm sure the cubs are ours. My lion-trainer reported the disappearance of three young lions a short while ago."

He and the Bobbseys rushed to the car. K. T.

peered inside the crate. "I can't be positive," he said. "But my trainer will know." He and Sam lifted the box.

K. T. hailed a passing workman and had him carry the cubs to the menagerie tent. There the lion-trainer identified the animals beyond a doubt.

"Beats me how they got away," the man declared. "Thanks for capturing them."

K. T. then invited the Bobbseys and Mr. Allen to his office trailer. When everyone was seated in comfortable wicker chairs, he smiled at Bert and Freddie. "I'm indebted to the twins for the second time today," he stated, telling of the boys' help in calming Dolly the elephant that morning. "I just can't understand how the cubs got to the vicinity of the lumberyard. It's a mystery, just like so many other things around here."

Mr. Allen spoke up. "Something bothering you, Ken? My men brought over your new tents in time, so I know it isn't that."

The circus owner hesitated, then said, "Our circus has been having all kinds of trouble lately."

"Like the fire in Marymont?" Bert asked.

K. T. nodded. "Yes," he replied. "And costumes have been disappearing, only to turn up later in unexpected places."

He added that several times in the past two

weeks poles supporting the tents had broken in two, although they had been fairly new. "I'm afraid our circus is jinxed!" K. T. concluded sadly.

"Have you any enemies who might want to cause you trouble?" Mr. Bobbsey asked.

K. T. shook his head. "Not that I know of. If I had any definite evidence, I'd call in the police. But I'd hate to get bad publicity in the papers about the Happy Top."

The Bobbseys offered to give the circus-owner any help he might need. K. T. said he would call on them if necessary, and thanked them wholeheartedly.

"We Bobbseys had better leave," said the twins' father, rising from his chair. "Your mother," he told Bert and Freddie, jokingly, "will think we've run into a lion!"

They drove to the church to pick up Mrs. Bobbsey, and the boys told her and Sam, who had been in the car when K. T. confided in them, about the mysterious happenings at the Happy Top. "Sounds like some snake-in-the-grass is tryin' to get even with K. T. Duncan," Sam remarked.

"But he doesn't have any enemies," Bert remarked.

Mrs. Bobbsey too thought someone had a grudge against the circus-owner. "It's a shame," she said.

As the car pulled into the Bobbseys' drive, Nan and Flossie ran outside to meet the arrivals. "We've been capturing lions!" Freddie proudly told his sisters.

Flossie and Nan were astonished and at the same time overjoyed to see Snoop. After hearing of the mysterious happenings at the circus, the girls looked serious.

"Maybe we can find some clue," Nan said.

"Let's try," Bert proposed.

They entered the house and found Dinah puffing breathlessly in the kitchen. "Been chasing Waggo all over this house," she said, trying to look indignant, but chuckling instead.

Sam, who loved to tease his wife, winked at the Bobbseys. "Waggo was probably showing Dinah a new trick," he said.

"Humph!" Dinah exclaimed. "A brownie-snatchin' trick. Stood right up on his hind legs —Waggo did—and sneaked three of them off the kitchen table!" Flossie giggled, and the others grinned.

Then Mr. Bobbsey said to the twins, "Since Mr. Riker hasn't claimed Waggo, I think we'd better put an ad in the Lost-and-Found section of the newspaper."

Flossie and Freddie were crestfallen. They had been hoping secretly that Waggo might become another of their pets, and a permanent friend for Snap and Snoop.

"But I guess his master wants him," Flossie sighed. Her father said he would call in the ad in the morning.

The day had been a busy one and the twins were ready for sleep when bedtime came. But in the early morning hours, Nan, who shared a room with Flossie, was wakened by a tug on her arm.

"Nan! Nan!" her small sister said in an urgent voice from the next bed. "Waggo and Snap are barking!"

Rubbing her eyes sleepily, Nan yawned. "They're all right," she told Flossie. "Go back to sleep."

But Flossie insisted that the dogs were having trouble. "Please come and look with me," she begged.

Nan got out of bed, knowing Flossie would not go back to sleep until she was reassured. They stepped into their slippers and put on light robes, then tiptoed to the darkened first floor. Nan led the way to the kitchen and opened the back door. All was quiet now, but Nan felt something brush against her leg. Startled, she jumped back.

"Oh!" she exclaimed.

Flossie and Nan heard a purring sound and began to giggle. "It's Snoop!" Nan said. "He thinks it's time for his breakfast milk."

She picked up the cat and the sisters looked

out the window. They glimpsed a shadowy figure slinking around their garage!

Both girls rushed upstairs and wakened their parents and brothers by shouting, "Come quickly, everybody!" As the bedroom doors opened, Nan told what she and Flossie had seen. The parents and the boys grabbed their slippers and robes and raced to the kitchen.

"Let's call the police, Dick!" suggested Mrs. Bobbsey.

Her husband replied that first they should determine whether or not there actually was a prowler nearby. He switched on the outdoor floodlight. Instantly the back yard was brightly illuminated. No one was in sight.

Mr. Bobbsey said he would check the garage. Freddie and Bert went with him, and Nan, Flossie, and Mrs. Bobbsey kept watch from the house.

Mr. Bobbsey and the boys walked all around the garage with their flashlights, but saw no one. Snap greeted them with a friendly bark.

Bert shone his light around the pets' runway. "Hey! Where's Waggo?" he asked. He opened the latched door of the runway and peered inside the dog's house.

"It's empty!" he cried out.

CHAPTER X

MISSING!

"EMPTY!" Freddie cried in disbelief. "Why it can't be—I put Waggo to bed myself!"

Mr. Bobbsey and Freddie entered the run and saw that Bert was right. The terrier was gone!

"I don't understand this at all," Mr. Bobbsey stated as he beamed his flashlight around.

Freddie was testing the latch on the door to the run. "Waggo's smart, but even he couldn't open this by himself," the little boy declared.

Suddenly Bert's flash shone on something white and shiny clinging to a nearby bush. "Say, look here Dad," he said, plucking it off.

The object was a piece of waxed kitchen paper. Bert straightened it out and saw a reddish-brown scrap of meat sticking to the paper. "Chopped beef!" he cried.

"Someone must have persuaded Waggo to leave here by giving him meat," Mr. Bobbsey deduced.

At that moment Snap gave a sharp bark. Bert

turned to the shaggy dog. "If only you could tell us what happened to Waggo!" he said to the pet.

"I'll bet Snap got some meat too, to keep him busy while that person took Waggo. Anyway he did bark and give a warning."

At that moment Mrs. Bobbsey called from the house, "Have you found anything?"

Quickly Mr. Bobbsey and the boys returned and told the girls and Mrs. Bobbsey what had happened.

Flossie burst into tears. "Wh—who would steal dear little Waggo?" she wailed. "Who could be so mean?"

Freddie looked sober. "Mr. Riker would feel terrible about it, too," he said.

"If Waggo's not back by morning," said Mr. Bobbsey, "I'll call the police." He added that he would also report the figure Nan had seen at the garage.

The twins' mother urged everyone to return to bed. "Don't forget, the circus parade is to-morrow!"

The family went upstairs and soon the house was quiet again. But the small twins tossed restlessly in their sleep, worrying about Waggo. They were the first ones to hurry outside in the morning to the dog run. It was empty! The twins ran back into the house.

"Daddy!" Flossie cried. "Call the police-men!"

Instantly Mr. Bobbsey went to the phone and gave the police chief a full account of what had happened. The officer promised to do all he could to find Waggo.

When Flossie heard this, she became thoughtful. "Do you think maybe Danny Rugg took Waggo?" she asked.

Nan and Bert agreed this was possible. Perhaps Danny was still angry over the elephant incident at the Happy Top Circus. If he had learned that the Bobbseys were keeping Waggo, Danny might have taken the dog in order to get even.

"I'll go to Danny's house and find out!" Bert declared. "There's time before the circus parade starts."

Nan offered to join Bert. Flossie and Freddie wanted to go to Danny's also, but Bert said it would look less suspicious if only two went.

After breakfast the older twins started out. When they reached the Ruggs' home, they went around to the back yard to see if Waggo were tied there. The dog was not in sight. Nan and Bert hid behind a large tree and looked about cautiously.

"Let's search the garage," Nan whispered.

"Okay," said Bert. "But let's be quiet."

The two crept toward the garage. As they were about to enter it, the twins heard whistling. Then the back door of the house opened and

Danny walked into the yard. He was carrying a large wooden box.

When he saw Nan and Bert, he demanded rudely, "What are you Bobbseys doing, sneaking around our garage?" Danny set the wooden box on the ground and faced the twins defiantly.

Bert told Danny about Waggo's disappearance. "He's a black-and-white terrier," Bert added, "and we think he might've wandered off and got lost."

"I don't know anything about a dog named Waggo," Danny retorted. "You've got a nerve. What makes you think he's in my yard? I didn't take him!"

"We didn't accuse you, Danny," Nan said quickly.

At this, Danny's face turned beet red. "Well, I wouldn't touch any of your flea-bitten pets!" he cried unpleasantly. "Now go home!"

Disgusted with the bully's bad manners, Nan and Bert started to turn away. But Nan, eyeing the wooden box, paused to ask:

"What's in the box, Danny?"

"Oh, something special," Danny replied slyly, a gleam of mischief coming into his eyes. "I'll show you. It's not a dog either," he taunted.

Danny came up to the twins and pressed a spring which released the lid of the box. "See!" he said triumphantly.

Out jumped a large, olive-colored toad with

bulging eyes! With a loud croak, the toad landed
on Nan's arm then jumped to the ground.

Nan's first impulse had been to shriek when
the toad touched her. But the girl realized
Danny was hoping to frighten her, and forced
herself to smile.

"How adorable!" she cried gaily. "Look,
Bert!"

She pointed toward the toad which was hopping across the grass. Her brother grinned.
"Better catch your pet, Danny, or he'll get
away."

Then he and Nan, feeling certain that if

Waggo were at Danny's, they'd never be able to prove it, left for home. The younger twins ran to meet them. "Any luck?" Flossie asked eagerly.

"No."

Though Flossie and Freddie were disappointed about Waggo, they laughed on hearing of Danny's attempted toad scare. Then Freddie said proudly, "I called the dog warden while you were gone. He'll be on the lookout for Waggo."

A short while later the Bobbseys left for the circus parade. Since it was Saturday, Mr. Bobbsey could enjoy the parade too without having to take time off from business. But Charlie Mason had called to say he could not attend the circus that day. He had to go with his parents on an out-of-town trip.

When the twins and their parents reached the center of town, where the parade was to be held, they looked for a good place on the sidewalk from which to view the spectacle. Many other Lakeport families were also reserving places.

"I see a spot!" cried Nan, darting toward an empty space along the nearby curb. The other Bobbseys followed, and agreed that it was indeed an ideal location.

"Look here!" Mrs. Bobbsey pointed to a raised block of stone on the sidewalk.

"It's an old carriage stone," the twins' father observed.

"What's that?" asked Freddie, as he examined the stone, which stood about three feet high.

Mr. Bobbsey explained that in the horse-and-buggy days, the steppingstone had been used by Lakeport ladies to climb in and out of their carriages.

"This'll be a swell place for Flossie and me to stand," Freddie said, helping his sister up onto the stone and climbing up after her. Flossie held her favorite doll, Jane, in her arms. Now she playfully set the doll on her shoulders.

Bert chuckled. "Jane can see better than anybody."

The parade started a short while later. Red-coated musicians playing shiny brass instruments and beating large drums marched briskly down the street. How jolly their lively tunes sounded!

"Here come the clowns!" Flossie cried happily.

Dressed in gaudy billowing costumes, the lovable clowns cavorted down the street. Their faces were daubed in green, blue, yellow, and red paint. Some clowns wore funny, floppy wigs, while others had silly hats perched on their heads. All wore awkward, flapping shoes.

"Hello! Hello!" they called to the clapping children, throwing kisses left and right.

Mr. Bobbsey pointed out two clowns who were dressed alike in green, polka-dotted suits. They were pretending to play fake tin horns. After them came a hobo clown chasing a dwarf-sized clown with a rubber football.

"Hi, Gee-Gee!" chorused the Bobbsey twins. With a huge grin the clown waved as he passed.

Next came trucks with roofs and heavy bars on the sides. The wild animals! There were several tigers and lions, two hippopotamuses, one leopard, and a black panther. Behind the trucks were two camels with humps on their backs.

"They're Humpty-dumpty camels!" Flossie giggled.

Freddie nodded. He liked the men who were riding them. They were dressed like desert Arabs with long white cloaks and turbans on their heads.

Suddenly a little girl cried out, "Here come the elephants!"

The Bobbseys looked down the street. The huge beasts swung slowly into view, with several trainers to keep them in line. Each elephant's name was printed on a velvet mantle hanging over its back.

"There's Dolly!" cried Flossie. "Hi, Dolly! Hi, Dolly!" she yelled, waving at the elephant as she drew abreast of the twins.

Dolly the elephant stopped short as she heard her name called, almost causing the elephant behind to bump into her. She swung her trunk around and looked at Flossie.

"She remembers me!" Flossie exclaimed with delight. Freddie told his twin to hold her doll Jane up high, so Dolly could see her.

Flossie did this. Slowly, the elephant came closer, despite her trainer's efforts to keep her in line. Suddenly Dolly extended her long trunk toward Flossie. The little girl's eyes blinked with amazement, as the elephant's trunk curled around Jane and lifted her from Flossie's hand. As the elephant turned to continue in the parade, Flossie cried loudly:

"Save my Jane! Dolly is taking her away!"

CHAPTER XI

FAT-LADY FLOSSIE

"DON'T worry, Flossie! I'll rescue your doll!" Bert cried, dashing into the street.

Meanwhile, Dolly the elephant had lumbered back to her place in line. She was holding Flossie's "Jane" very gently but proudly in her curled-under trunk. Many people were laughing and children were clapping. But Flossie did not think it was so funny.

Bert spied the head elephant-trainer, Amos, in the line-up and hurried to the gray-haired man's side.

"Can you stop the elephants for a minute?" he asked.

The trainer, looking annoyed, shook his head. "No I can't!" he replied curtly. "I have to keep the parade line moving!"

"I know, but my sister's doll—" Bert began, pointing to the playful elephant.

"Get it later!" Amos snapped and flicked his

switch across the legs of a nearby elephant.

"Wait a minute! Stop the parade!" yelled a good-natured spectator who had heard the conversation. "There's a tiny lady in distress!"

"Yeah, mister, don't be an old lemon!" a teenaged youth called out.

The elephant-trainer's face turned red. In an angry voice he commanded several helpers to halt the elephants and walked over to Dolly.

"Give me that toy!" he demanded.

Dolly gave a trumpeting sound and stomped her right leg impatiently. Jane's blue glass eyes blinked open and shut with the motion.

Amos repeated the order impatiently and the big elephant eyed him calmly but did not lower the doll. The trainer lifted his whip, about to give the beast a crack on her flanks.

"Please don't hit her," Bert begged. "Let me try."

"All right, Mister Big Stuff!" the man scoffed. "If you're so smart, let's see what you can do!"

Bert reached in his pocket for some peanuts he had bought earlier for the small twins. Holding them out in his hand he said, "Please, Dolly, give me Flossie's toy—"

The elephant hesitated, evidently torn between a desire to keep the toy or munch on her favorite treat. Finally she lowered her trunk, placed Jane in Bert's left hand, and grabbed the peanuts from his right.

"Thank you, Dolly!" Bert said, grinning.

The spectators gave Bert a rousing cheer as he returned to his family. Amos, with a furious look on his face because Bert had accomplished what he had not, gave a terse command to "march!"

Flossie rewarded her brother with a big hug and cuddled her doll. "I'll watch you better from now on, Janie," she promised.

The parade continued. Many more colorful floats and another circus band passed the Bobbseys.

"There's Mr. Stilts!" cried Flossie as Stretch, the stunt man, strutted by and waved to her.

Finally the sound of merry-go-round-type music could be heard. Nan tapped her feet in time to the tinkling notes of the catchy tune.

"I think it's the calliope," her mother said.

Around the corner came the gaily decorated calliope. The small pipe organ was mounted on a truck. It was painted bright yellow and red. A man sat on the bench in front of the keyboard.

"That's the end of the parade," said Mr. Bobbsey, as the vehicle went on down the street and the crowd began to break up.

After a quick lunch at home, the Bobbseys walked to the Happy Top Circus grounds. Mr. Bobbsey bought tickets for himself and his wife, and the twins gave their free passes to the ticket-taker.

The four children looked around excitedly.

There was so much to see, and crowds of people were milling everywhere.

"*Balloons!— Freshly-roasted peanuts— Popcorn!— Cotton Candy—*" were the cries from the various vendors.

Flossie and Freddie paused before a souvenir stand on which stood many colorful toys.

Mrs. Bobbsey laughed. "Each of you may have something," she said.

The small twins looked over the selection of cowboy belts, toy clowns, pennants, parasols, stuffed animals, birds on a stick, and tin horns.

"I'll take this rubber clown doll with the funny face," Flossie finally decided.

Freddie chose a brown-leather cowboy belt studded with fake rubies, and fastened it around his waist. Nan and Bert took circus pennants.

"I'm going to call my new doll Bubu!" said Flossie, as Mr. Bobbsey paid the vendor.

"And I'm a real Western hero now!" Freddie exclaimed, and stuck his thumbs importantly between his chubby waist and the belt.

The family moved on and Mrs. Bobbsey suggested they visit the side shows. These were held in a smaller tent than the one for the regular performance. As they entered, Bert whispered in Nan's ear:

"I hope I get a chance later on to look over Mr. Rett's dogs."

His twin nodded, realizing that Bert wondered whether the unfriendly dog-trainer had anything to do with Waggo's disappearance. H had seemed anxious to obtain the trick terrier fo his show.

Just then the Bobbseys' attention was drawn to an announcer who was walking around a raised platform on which the "freaks," as he called them, were seated.

"And here, ladies and gentlemen," the tall husky man was saying in his microphone, "we have the only wild man in captivity—half man, half wolf!"

"G-r-r-r-r!" the wild man growled at the audience.

He had thick tangled brown hair, a large muscular body, and was dressed cave-man style in what appeared to be a leopard hide.

"I don't like him," Flossie whispered, holding tightly to Nan's hand.

The announcer walked on to the next exhibit. "Over here, folks, is the Wee-Tots Revue," he cried. "Six of the smallest folks in creation!"

"The midgets!" Nan said, and spotted the familiar face of their friend Teeny. All the twins waved.

After telling the audience that these little people were much older than they looked, the announcer introduced them. There were the men, Teeny, Weeny and Beany—

"And we're Queenie, Leenie, and Jeanie!"

chorused the velvet-gowned lady midgets, smiling endearingly at the spectators.

As the crowd started toward the next platform, Teeny motioned to Nan. She walked over to the midget's platform. Teeny bent down and thrust something into her hands. It was an autographed picture of the midget family.

"Why thank you!" Nan said, looking pleased. "This'll be a wonderful souvenir."

After talking to the midgets for a few minutes, Nan walked back toward her mother. Mrs. Bobbsey had waited near the platform, while Mr. Bobbsey, Bert, and the small twins had gone to see the Rubber Man maneuver his body into strange positions.

"Where's Flossie?" Nan asked. The other members of the family looked around and realized the little girl was not in sight.

"Don't tell me she's lost again!" Mrs. Bobbsey sighed.

Nan, who was sure her sister had not gone far, suggested that she and her mother walk around the large circular platform. As they rounded the corner, Nan heard a familiar voice.

"Oh, Nan—Mother—look at me!"

Flossie was seated on a tiny chair placed on the fat lady's platform!

An amused audience was chuckling at the sight of the small girl selling pictures of Daisy Dimples!

"Why Flossie!" Mrs. Bobbsey gasped. "How did you get up there?"

"I climbed all by myself," her daughter said proudly. "I'm learning how to be a fat lady."

Daisy Dimples shook with laughter and said, "She'll change her mind. Sometimes being fat is a nuisance. Why, I can't even fit into a movie seat!"

Just then Mr. Bobbsey, Bert, and Freddie walked up. Flossie's father laughed heartily and lifted his daughter to the ground.

"Time for the show in the Big Top," Bert reminded the family.

A few minutes later the Bobbseys were seated in an excellent location overlooking the center ring of the arena. The small twins gazed around at the maze of wires inside the tent.

Suddenly Nan nudged Bert. "Look!" she said in a low voice.

Danny Rugg was seated directly in front of the older twins!

At the same time, the twins saw Danny turn around, but when he saw them, he turned back quickly as if he didn't want the Bobbseys to know he had seen them.

Nan and Bert winked at each other.

Freddie opened his circus program. "Now we can learn what's in Jack Horner's pie!" he said.

At that moment a vendor carrying a basket of paper cones filled with pink fluff walked up the aisle steps. "Cotton Candy! Cotton Candy!" he sang out.

Freddie gazed wistfully at the light-as-air sweet. "Boy, that looks good, Daddy!" he said.

Mr. Bobbsey chuckled. He hailed the vendor and bought six cones.

"Mm-mm!" Flossie exclaimed as she licked the feathery candy. "This is almost like eating nothing, but it's fun."

"Oh," Nan said suddenly, "Nellie Parks and Grace Lavine are sitting over there." She stood up and waved to her two chums.

With his free right hand, Bert waved also. The twins and their friends called greetings to one another. At the same moment, the circus performers and band members took their places to begin the grand entry parade. Two clowns were walking up to a large cannon at one end of the large arena.

Suddenly the cannon exploded with a loud BOOM! A fake clown shot from its mouth and zoomed high—high up into the rafters of the tent.

Excitedly Bert started to point at the flying figure. But as he raised his arm, the cone of sticky cotton candy landed directly in Danny Rugg's hair!

CHAPTER XII

A LAUGHABLE EXPLOSION

DANNY RUGG looked as if he were wearing a peppermint wig, for Bert's cotton-candy cone was perched like a clown hat on top of his head!

Nan tried not to giggle and Bert said, "Oh, I'm sorry, Danny. I—"

The rest of Bert's apology was drowned out by the blare of bugles as the band started to lead the parade around the large circus ring.

As the Happy Top performers, mounted on their gaily decorated horses, began the colorful procession, Danny put his hand to his head.

"Ugh!" he exclaimed, as his fingers touched the candy. He whirled around. "Bert Bobbsey!" he yelled furiously. "You did this on purpose!"

"He did not!" Nan said indignantly. "It was an accident!"

Danny pulled the cone from his head, but little wisps of pink candy still clung to his dark hair.

Danny stood up, clenching his fists. "I'll fix you!" He glared at Bert.

Bert met the challenge, also rising. "I didn't do it on purpose, but just the same it serves you right for knocking over Flossie's and Freddie's orangeade stand!" he retorted.

"Down in front!" cried an annoyed spectator several rows in back of the boys.

Without warning Danny suddenly grabbed hold of Bert's right leg. The boy's knees buckled and he lost his balance, falling sideways into the aisle.

As Nan screamed, her twin tumbled head over heels, landing in a heap on the aisle step two rows ahead. A startled man sitting on the end got up quickly.

"Are you hurt, sonny?" he asked, assisting Bert to his feet.

"I—I guess not," Bert stammered. "It knocked the wind out of me, though."

By this time Mr. and Mrs. Bobbsey and Nan had rushed down the steps.

Bert grinned reassuringly. "I'm all right, Mother," he said, noting the worried look on her face.

"Thank goodness!" Mrs. Bobbsey exclaimed.

Mr. Bobbsey was angry at Danny's action and said so. He looked back at the place where Danny had been seated but the boy had vanished.

"I'm okay, so let's forget him for now," Bert

urged, not wanting to miss any more of the circus fun.

The four Bobbseys returned to their seats. By now the Grand Parade was over, and the first acts were starting in the three ground-level rings. Each ring was filled with a different colored tanbark—yellow in the main one, with pink and purple in the smaller adjoining rings.

"I don't know where to look first!" Flossie cried, her eyes darting from side to side. "And please, may Freddie and I sit in the aisle seats so we can see better?" Mr. Bobbsey nodded and the exchange of seats was made.

While two trained tigers were jumping through hoops in the center ring, three seals were balancing balls on their noses in the left one. In the third ring ten black and white French poodles were jumping through hoops held high. Then the dogs formed a pyramid.

Freddie watched with rapt attention as these acts were replaced shortly by nimble Japanese tumblers and men and women jugglers on roller skates.

"I'm going to try that," Freddie declared.

"And go kerplunk!" said Flossie.

Suddenly a group of clowns came running into the arena. All were of different heights and shapes, and wore even funnier costumes than they had in the morning parade.

"I see Gee-Gee!" Freddie called out.

The clown wore a suit with huge green polka dots, and pretended to run away from a taller clown holding a tiny club in one hand. He had on bright-blue pants, a short jacket, and a bow tie which lighted up first red, then green. On his head was a tiny yellow hat.

"Don't hit me! Don't hit me!" Gee-Gee cried in a squeaky voice as the tall clown gained on him and threateningly shook the tiny club.

The children in the big tent roared with laughter as Gee-Gee leaped over a rope in front of the first row of seats. The tall clown followed him to a place in the aisle directly alongside Flossie and Freddie. There before the eyes of the startled twins, Gee-Gee began to swell up like a balloon.

"Oh, Gee-Gee's going to pop like bubble gum!" Flossie cried fearfully.

Just then the taller clown raised his tiny club and wham! Gee-Gee fell over onto the steps. There was a loud hissing noise as his clown suit deflated.

"Oh, he must've been wearing a special balloon underneath," said Flossie in relief.

Mrs. Bobbsey nodded and commented, "It's amazing the way circus performers know how to fall without getting hurt. Gee-Gee's act certainly looked as if it weren't planned, but of course it was."

After the tall clown had struck Gee-Gee, he

had hurried up the aisle past the Bobbseys' seats and out an exit. But Gee-Gee still lay on the ground.

Next, two men dressed as hospital attendants, but wearing clown make-up, walked from a side exit carrying a stretcher. Making funny faces at the audience, they came up to Gee-Gee, leaned down and felt his pulse. Then they lifted the clown onto the stretcher and bore him outside.

"Gee-Gee's certainly a good actor!" Nan declared.

The twins' attention was soon diverted to other exciting acts in the center ring. A pretty blond-haired woman, billed as the "Princess of the High-Wire," was walking across a pencil-thin wire. She held only a fan in her outstretched hand for balance. Then a man rode a bicycle across the same wire.

"Phew!" Bert exclaimed. "How does he keep from falling off?" His father said it took years of training to learn this stunt.

The high-wire act was followed by one in which a man and a woman did amusing tricks on one-wheeled bicycles. Then Jandy, Jimmy, and Carla Duncan came into the center ring to do their acrobatic stunts.

The Bobbseys cheered lustily for their friends. "They're wonderful!" cried Flossie, when the trio completed the act to thunderous applause.

The trumpets blared loudly as the center ring was cleared. The Bobbseys consulted their programs to see what the next Happy Top attraction would be.

"Yippee!" Freddie sang out. "The Jack-Horner Pie!"

A large flap was opened at one end of the huge tent and the children saw a spectacular float being drawn in by a dozen snow-white horses. Red-spangled saddles lay on their backs and each wore a high plumed hat. The horses pranced into the arena.

The sides of the float were covered with red and gold glitter. On the center of the float stood a gigantic pie. Topped with a gleaming gold crust, the pie stood in a silver "dish," about fifty feet around.

"Oo-oo!" Flossie cried with delight. "It's too bee-yoo-tiful to eat."

"It sure is," said Bert.

The huge Jack Horner Pie was pulled into the center of the ring. The horses halted and men dressed in black suits ran toward the float. They climbed up onto the platform and grabbed hold of long wires which were being lowered from the ceiling. They attached the wires to various sections of the Jack Horner Pie.

"Hey! They're going to open the pie," Freddie bounced up and down excitedly in his seat.

A fanfare of music rang through the arena as the men jumped to the ground.

"You're right, Freddie," said Nan. "Look!"

As if by magic, the wires began to pull up sections of the golden crust. An awed hush fell over the crowd.

On the under side of each "slice" of the pie was a handle. Holding onto this was a man or woman wearing a gold-and-white sequined costume!

"They're aerialists!" Bert exclaimed, as the Bobbseys watched the figures, twelve in all, gracefully rising from the immense silver dish.

"And now, ladies and gentlemen," came the announcer's voice over the loud-speaker, "we will see the world-famous Deloros Dozen, who will perform specialty numbers never before seen in the United States!"

Meanwhile, the twelve aerialists, each of whom had a tiny bag tied around his waist, had swung themselves down from the float, and went to climb up other wires attached to various trapezes.

When they reached the high swings, they rocked back and forth in couples. Smiling to the crowd below, they opened the bags and tossed little objects to people in the audience.

"A prize!" Freddie shouted.

He hoped to catch one, but it was Bert who caught a package. Quickly he opened it. Inside was a huge candy in the shape of a pie. Bert broke it into six pieces and all the Bobbseys enjoyed the treat.

"It's yummy," Nan declared.

By now the performance had started. First the acrobats crossed from one bar to another in mid air. Then they held onto a high-swinging trapeze by just a foot or an arm.

When the Deloros' exhibition was over, Nan exclaimed, "Oh! I was *so* afraid one of the people would fall. I didn't even dare breathe!"

"Me, too!" her twin admitted.

Since it was now intermission, Mrs. Bobbsey suggested that they go to the menagerie tent and look at the rest of the side shows.

"Yes, let's," Freddie said eagerly. "I want to see the big gorillas!"

"And the giraffes," Bert added.

The family went outside the main tent and a few minutes later entered the animal tent. Bert saw Jimmy Duncan standing near the entrance. Excusing himself, he went to speak to his circus friend. Jimmy was talking with a clown and looked worried. As Bert approached, Jimmy pointed to an exit and the clown hurried off.

"Hi, Bert!" Jimmy said, looking grave.

"What's wrong?" Bert asked instantly.

Jimmy hesitated, then replied. "Something terrible has happened!"

"What?"

Lowering his voice to a whisper, Jimmy said, "Do you remember when Gee-Gee fell to the ground after being struck by a tall clown?"

"Sure do," Bert replied. "Gee-Gee's a terrific stunt man, some act he put on!"

"Yes," Jimmy agreed, "but that tall clown wasn't part of the act, Bert. We don't know who he was or why he did it, but he really knocked Gee-Gee unconscious!"

CHAPTER XIII

FREDDIE A HERO

BERT was shocked to learn that Gee-Gee had been intentionally knocked out by the tall clown. "Will he be all right?" he asked Jimmy.

"We hope so, Bert. The person struck him with a real club—not the hollow rubber ones usually used."

The circus boy said his father and the doctor were with the clown now. Gee-Gee had regained consciousness and luckily had no broken bones or other injuries. But he must rest for a while.

"Could he identify the tall clown who struck him?" Bert asked.

Jimmy shook his head. "No, but we think the man is someone who works for the circus. Dad told me that the costume the tall clown had on wasn't supposed to be worn today. It's missing from the wardrobe room. And only performers can go in there."

"We thought the chasing scene was part of the

act," Bert said thoughtfully. "And when the stretcher-bearers came out and made funny faces we were sure of it."

Jimmy explained that many times the clowns would make up tricks on the spur of the moment. Gee-Gee had said when the tall man started to chase him, he had played along with the performance.

But when Gee-Gee fell, everyone backstage knew something was wrong. To keep the audience calm, the clown stretcher-bearers were sent to get Gee-Gee.

Bert nodded, impressed by the game spirit of these circus people. They helped one another, and would keep their show going no matter how worried they were. "Does Gee-Gee have any enemies?" he asked.

"I don't think so," Jimmy replied, adding that Gee-Gee had worked for the Happy Top Circus only a short time, but seemed to be well liked.

Just then Nan joined the two boys. Jimmy greeted her, then excused himself and hurried out the exit. Bert quickly told Nan what had happened.

"Oh, poor poor Gee-Gee!" Nan exclaimed. "And K. T., too. His circus is certainly having bad luck!"

The older twins caught up with the other Bobbseys. Freddie was peering at a white polar bear. Flossie stared in fascination at a reddish-orange, shaggy-haired wild ape from Borneo. Mr. and Mrs. Bobbsey stood nearby.

"I like that orange-tang best!" Flossie told Nan and pointed at the wild ape.

Her sister chuckled. "That animal is called an orangutan, Flossie," she said.

The Bobbseys walked on through the menagerie tent. There were blue-faced baboons, South American jaguars, a rhinoceros, lions, and elephants. The twins spoke to Dolly, who swung her trunk to and fro.

Bert laughed. "It's said elephants never forget. I guess Dolly knows us."

"Now we'd better return to our seats," Mrs. Bobbsey said. "It's time for the second half of the circus." The family trooped back to the main arena and found their places.

The small twins watched with interest as a truck bearing a small model house drove into the center ring. While the house was being unloaded, Mr. Rett's dog act came into the right-hand ring and a trained horse number started up in the left one.

"Let's look for Waggo," Nan whispered to Bert.

Intent on the dogs, the older twins did not notice that clouds of smoke and red flame were coming from the roof of the small model house. Then an arm extended from one of the second-floor windows clutching a white bundle.

"Help! Help! Save my baby!" came a cry.

"The house is on fire!" Freddie cried instantly. "And someone's trapped inside!"

Before anyone could stop him, the small boy was running down the steps toward the ground.

Bert forgot all about the dog act. "I'll get Freddie!" he yelled and darted after his younger brother, with the other twins following.

But Freddie, with a head start, was already in the arena, racing toward the center ring. Just then a miniature fire engine holding six midgets dressed in firemen suits clanged past Freddie.

"I'm a *real* fireman!" the blond-haired boy cried to the driver. "Let me come with you!"

"Okay, hop on!" said the driver to Freddie, and he stopped the engine while one of the midgets gave the little boy a hand. Then the little engine charged up to the burning house.

All the midgets jumped to the ground and started to unload fire-fighting equipment. One handed Freddie a long hose. "Aim it!" he directed.

"It works just like my toy fire-engine hose," thought Freddie, squirting a stream of water toward the second story.

At the same moment the white bundle was tossed from the upper window. A fireman caught it and said, "It's the baby—but don't worry!"

Freddie took a closer look and saw that the

baby was a rubber doll. The house on fire was only a circus act!

When the "fire" was out and the "smoke" had cleared away, three sides of the house were lowered to the ground. In the middle of the tiny building sat Daisy Dimples, the fat lady!

Slowly, she got to her feet and walked over to Freddie. "My hero!" she cried, and the entire audience roared with laughter and clapped loudly.

Freddie had to laugh, too. "I was really fooled," he said to Daisy.

Nevertheless, the little boy felt pleased at having helped put out a fire, even though it was only for fun! He was given a ride around the arena on the fire engine, and then clanged up to the side exit where Mr. Bobbsey and Bert were waiting. Freddie waved good-by to the small firemen. Then he and his father returned to their seats.

Bert, in the meantime, had remained behind and was now walking outside the performance tent. It had occurred to him that this might be a good time to get a closer look at Mr. Rett's dogs, whose act had ended. When he reached the animal-trainer's tent, Bert called the man's name. There was no reply.

Surprised, Bert entered the tent and quickly glanced at the cages. There were poodles, boxers, and a few terriers. But Waggo was not one of them. Disappointed, Bert returned to his seat and told Nan.

"I guess we'll have to forget our suspicions about Mr. Rett having anything to do with Waggo," Nan whispered.

The circus ended in a grand finale, with all the performers marching around the arena dressed in glittering pink-and-black costumes. They bowed and waved to the audience in time to the rousing tattoo of the drums.

"Oh, it was all just wonderful—every second!" Nan exclaimed as the Bobbseys left their seats and headed once more for the side-show tent. The others agreed heartily.

The first attraction they saw was Zingo, the sword-swallower. He was dressed in a gold-colored suit and held two shining blades. While the Bobbseys watched wide-eyed, he thrust both swords down his throat at the same time!

Flossie grimaced and turned her head, but Freddie said, "Boy! How does he do that?"

Bert shook his head. "I don't know. He makes sword-swallowing seem as easy as brushing teeth," he said.

"Look over there!" cried Freddie.

He pointed to a platform on which a man was advertised as the tallest in the world. Bert grinned. "Here's a real giant, Flossie."

His small sister looked at the giant with awe.

His height was announced as eight feet nine inches.

"He's a space man already," Bert said with a chuckle.

In a little while Mrs. Bobbsey noted that it was close to suppertime. The family left the tent and walked home. In their living room, Bert told the others about Gee-Gee's mysterious attacker.

"Oh!" cried Flossie, shocked. *"Who* would want to hurt Gee-Gee?"

Nan shook her head sadly. "I can't imagine. But whoever struck Gee-Gee knew he could probably make a safe getaway in all the noise and confusion."

"I wish I could find that fake tall clown," Bert stated. "He might be the one behind the rest of K. T.'s circus troubles."

At this moment Dinah called from the kitchen, saying that Sam had set up a surprise for them in the back yard.

"Last one's a snail!" cried Freddie.

He raced into the kitchen followed by Nan, Bert, and Flossie. They found Dinah looking out a rear window.

"There!" the cook beamed, pointing.

The children shouted with joy. In the lot behind the garage they could see a big white tent topped with an American flag!

"Wow!" exclaimed Freddie. "Our own circus tent!"

The twins dashed out the door into the yard. Mr. and Mrs. Bobbsey, smiling, followed. Sam, a wide grin on his face, stood near the tent. He said it had been delivered early that afternoon.

"Thanks millions for putting it up," Nan said to Sam. "Oh, what a gorgeous tent!"

"It's a dandy!" Bert cried.

Freddie was already inside the tent. The others quickly joined him.

"I'll bet we can fit twenty people in here," Freddie declared, glancing happily about the spacious interior. Flossie walked around and around. Suddenly she ran to hug her father.

"Oh Daddy!" she exclaimed. "This is the *most* bee-yoo-ti-ful present in the world!"

Sam spoke up with a chuckle. "Guess you're all set for *your* circus now."

"That's right." Nan nodded eagerly.

Before supper, the twins gathered on the porch and began discussing plans for their backyard circus. Freddie announced he would do a fire-fighting act with his toy fire engine as part of his performance.

"Freddie's going to use my doll house and rescue one of my dolls," Flossie piped up.

"You're not going to start a fire!" Nan exclaimed.

Freddie looked serious. "I wouldn't really set fire to Flossie's doll house," he promised. "It would be make-believe."

Bert said he had decided to do a tumbling act with Charlie Mason.

"And I'm going to be the fat lady," Flossie decided promptly.

Everyone laughed. Then Bert asked Nan, "What're you going to do, Sis?"

Looking mysterious, Nan replied that her circus act would be a surprise. No one could get the slightest hint from her. But she did say, "We'll have to start teaching Snoop and Snap tricks."

"If we only had Waggo here, we could have a swell dog act," Freddie said wistfully.

Mr. Bobbsey told his small son that he and Flossie should try not to worry about Waggo. After all, perhaps the dog was back with his real owner.

"Unless," Bert thought, "Mr. Rett *does* have Waggo hidden somewhere." He resolved to ask Jimmy Duncan the next day if the trainer had acquired a new trick dog.

A chime sounded, telling the Bobbseys that supper was ready. All ate heartily. When Dinah came in with dessert, lemon sherbet and cookies, Freddie said to her:

"Dinah, I'm a circus sword-swallower!" He tilted his head back and lifted an imaginary sword to his mouth. "Gulp!" Freddie swallowed hard.

"Mercy!" the plump cook exclaimed and shut

her eyes tight. "Even the idea gives me the shivers."

Dinah, shaking her head, bustled toward the kitchen. Suddenly she stopped short and the Bobbseys sat bolt upright. A strange but familiar sound came to their ears.

"Rat-a-tat-tat! Rat-a-tat-tat!"

CHAPTER XIV

A FUNNY MIDGET

"WAGGO'S back!" Nan cried and hurried to the kitchen, expecting to see the black-and-white terrier. But the room was empty except for Snoop, who was lapping milk from a saucer near the sink.

Rat-tat-tat! Rat-tat-tat!

"It's coming from right outside the kitchen door," said Bert, and ran to look through the screen.

"But it's not Waggo." He pointed to a large oak near the door.

At the bottom of the tree trunk was a hollowed-out area. Inside this a dark-brown bird with yellow-shafted wings was sitting on a nest. Nearby, the father bird was pecking rapidly on the trunk.

"They're called flickers," observed Mrs. Bobbsey.

"Aren't they pretty!" Flossie cried out.

"Yes," Freddie said glumly. "But I wish it was Waggo."

The next day was Sunday. After church and dinner, the twins spent the afternoon trying to teach tricks to Snap and Snoop. By nightfall both children and animals were weary. But Nan said with satisfaction:

"At least Snap will roll over and walk on his hind legs when we signal and Snoop has learned to sit up pretty well."

Bert nodded. "If we saw the Happy Top Circus again, we could get some more ideas for ours."

"Oh, yes! Let's!" Flossie and Freddie chorused eagerly.

Nan sighed. "It would be fun. But I've spent most of my allowance this month. I don't have enough for a ticket."

The others admitted they, too, had little spending money left. "I know," Bert said, then talked in low tones with Nan and the small twins.

At breakfast the next morning, Bert looked at his mother with a twinkle in his eye. "Do you have any special jobs we might do for you today?" he asked her.

"Something we could earn money for?" Freddie added.

Mr. and Mrs. Bobbsey exchanged winks. "*Why* do you suppose the children want to earn money, Dick?" Mrs. Bobbsey asked her husband.

Mr. Bobbsey pretended to look very puzzled. "I can't imagine, Mary."

"Oh, Daddy, you're teasing," Flossie spoke up. "You know we've spent all our allowances and—and—"

"We'd love to see the Happy Top Circus once more," Nan finished with a coaxing smile. "We thought Dinah would like to go with us this time."

Dinah entered the room at this moment bearing a platter of crisp bacon.

"Why, that's sure nice of you, honey lambs," she said with appreciation. "But today I'm going to wash the downstairs windows. It'll take me quite a while."

"We'll all pitch in," Bert offered promptly. "We can have the windows done by lunchtime."

Mr. Bobbsey rose from the table. With a chuckle he drew out his wallet. "Sounds like a fair bargain." He handed Bert a bill and added, "Here's your pay in advance for five circus tickets and refreshments."

"Thank you, thank you," cried the twins.

Dinah beamed. "I'm right happy too. Seein' the circus will be a real treat."

Nan and Bert got pails and clean cloths. When Dinah and the older twins had washed the windows on the inside, the younger ones dried them. Soon each pane was sparkling clean.

After lunch, Dinah put on what she called her

"goin' out" clothes—a blue-print dress, large white hat, and comfortable summer shoes.

"We want to show you everything, Dinah," said Flossie, as they headed downtown.

As they entered the circus gate, Bert spotted Jandy and Jimmy Duncan walking toward them. The circus children hurried up to them and Nan introduced Dinah. Bert asked Jimmy whether Mr. Rett had obtained a new trick dog since the day before.

"I don't think so," replied Jimmy, adding that the dog-trainer had told his father that very morning he was still one dog short for his act. This definitely ruled out the possibility that Mr. Rett had stolen Waggo or had bought him from the thief.

Jimmy glanced at his watch. "Jandy, we have to get ready for the show," he reminded his sister. "Do you fellows want to come back to the men's dressing room with me?" he asked Bert and Freddie.

"You bet," said the two boys, thinking it would be interesting to watch the performers put on costumes and apply their make-up.

"Flossie and I will show Dinah the side show and menagerie tents while you're gone," said Nan. She told her brothers they would meet them at this same spot in about half an hour.

Nan, Flossie, and Dinah strolled around the two exhibits. When they stopped in front of

Daisy Dimples, the fat lady, Dinah exclaimed, "My oh my. She's even heftier than me."

Flossie introduced the cook to Daisy, who said with a hearty laugh, "You should've seen little Flossie helping me out Saturday."

Dinah laughed too, and the trio waved to Daisy as they moved on.

"Hmm," Nan said presently. "I wonder where the midgets are." She pointed to the platform, now vacant, where the little people had stood yesterday. Just then Flossie cried out, "Here they come now!"

Sure enough, through the tent entrance strutted the midgets.

"One-two-three-four-five-six-*seven!*" Flossie counted in amazement. "Why, yesterday there were only six midgets."

Suddenly one of the little men, wearing a top hat and cutaway, broke from the group and ran toward the Bobbseys.

"It must be Weeny!" said Nan, smiling.

"No, I think it's Beany!" Flossie guessed.

To both girls' amazement, however, the midget rushed up to Dinah. "Hi, Dinah!" he greeted her in a squeaky voice, pulling at his enormous black mustache.

Looking startled and mystified, Dinah said, "Hi, little man, what's your name?"

"Don't you really know?" the midget squeaked.

Dinah shook her head, more puzzled than ever. "I'm positive, or—should I?"

Suddenly the midget whipped off his shiny top hat, disclosing a head of curly blond hair!

"Oh!" Flossie shrieked. "Freddie Bobbsey! You're the seventh midget!"

She burst into gales of laughter, as did Dinah and Nan. Indeed, the little boy looked very comical. The fake mustache was so large it covered most of his round face.

Freddie's eyebrows had been made black with charcoal and his cheeks were reddened with make-up. Now he grinned widely and pulled off the mustache. "Dinah, you really thought I was a circus midget," he said.

"I sure did," Dinah chuckled, and the girls admitted they had been fooled too.

All this time the real midgets had looked on in great amusement. Teeny walked up and explained that when Freddie had visited the men's dressing room he had asked to borrow a costume from the midgets.

"Freddie's close to our size," Teeny continued, "so we thought it would be a good trick and helped him dress and put on make-up."

Just then Bert rushed up looking worried. "Where's Fred—?" he broke off in astonishment as he spotted his brother. Then with a grin he said, "Next time, Freddie, let a fellow know when you take off."

The two boys hurried away to the dressing room so Freddie could change into his own clothes. Nan suggested that Dinah and Flossie go to their seats. She would wait for her brothers.

"All right," agreed Flossie, who did not want to miss any of the performance. "It's almost time for the show to start."

Nan, while waiting for the boys, thought over the idea she had for a stunt in the children's circus. "I'll call Grace Lavine and Nellie Parks tonight and see if they'll do it with me," she thought.

Suddenly Nan's attention was drawn to several Happy Top people who were hurrying into the performer's entrance of the main tent. She saw a pretty girl in a yellow ballet costume, followed by a clown dressed as a tramp with a ragged coat, baggy pants, and a hobo's stick.

Then another clown bustled by. He wore a brown, shaggy costume resembling fur and had an imitation monkey head over his own. But instead of entering the main tent, this clown headed for the circus gate. As Nan watched, the clown changed his course and walked toward K. T. Duncan's office trailer.

"That's odd," Nan murmured.

At that moment Bert and Freddie appeared and the three children went to their seats. Flossie and Dinah were waiting. All thoughts of the clown-monkey were forgotten by Nan as the performance started.

The four twins loved the show just as much the second time as they had the first. They also enjoyed Dinah's excited comments and gasps of amazement at the daring stunts and colorful costumes. When the intermission was announced, Dinah suggested they all go outside and have some lemonade. "My treat this time," she added.

The twins agreed readily and, with Dinah, headed for the lemonade stand, which was near the main gate. As they stood sipping the refreshing fruit drink, Nan spotted K. T. Duncan entering his office trailer.

"There's the circus-owner," she told Dinah, pointing him out.

"Runnin' this circus must be a mighty big job," Dinah replied. "It—"

She broke off when K. T. Duncan suddenly flung open the door of the office trailer and shouted:

"I've been robbed!"

Everyone within hearing distance—children, their parents, circus workmen, vendors, and performers rushed up to the owner as he stepped to the ground.

The Bobbseys and Dinah had immediately left the lemonade stand and hurried along with the crowd. As they drew near K. T., they heard him say, "Money was taken from my office safe. The thief must have gotten into the trailer a short while ago. I was here until half an hour before intermission."

The circus-owner's face was lined with worry. He threw up his hands in despair. "Anybody here see the thief?" he called out to the crowd.

There was a brief silence, then a chorus of sympathetic "No's."

"Poor K. T." Nan sighed. "This circus really is jinxed!" she whispered to her twin. "Just like he told us the other day."

Bert shook his head and frowned. "I don't think it's any jinx. Some person is causing K.T. all this trouble for a reason. I've seen the safe. It has a big dial with a combination. That thief must be a pretty good safe-cracker."

Just then an odd expression crossed Nan's face, as if she had suddenly remembered something. "Oh!" she cried out.

The others looked at her startled. Mysteriously, Nan motioned them to follow her.

CHAPTER XV

A TIGHT-ROPE CAT

"WHAT is it, Nan?" Bert asked curiously, as the children and Dinah reached a secluded spot away from the rest of the crowd.

His sister told them about the monkey-headed clown she had seen walking toward K. T.'s trailer a short time before the circus performance had begun. "Do you think he could be the thief?" she asked.

"Yes, I do," Bert answered.

"A clue! A clue!" Freddie cried. "I wish we could catch him."

"We'd better tell K. T. anyway," Bert said. "There's a chance that the monkey-clown may be the same one who knocked Gee-Gee out yesterday."

He asked Nan whether the clown she had seen was as tall as the one who had struck Gee-Gee.

Nan thought a moment, but said she could not

138

be sure. "Let's go tell K. T. right now," she urged.

Flossie and Freddie were torn between wanting to solve the mystery and seeing the rest of the circus.

"There'll be more animal acts," Freddie said. "Some of 'em might be good tricks for Snap and Snoop."

Finally the small twins decided to return to their seats with Dinah, while Nan and Bert headed for the circus-owner's trailer.

Jimmy Duncan, looking troubled, opened the door at Bert's knock and greeted his friends. "Come in," he invited.

"We're so sorry to hear of the burglary," Nan said sympathetically.

Bert nodded. "Nan has something to tell your dad that might be a good clue," he added. "Is he here?"

"No, he went to police headquarters a few minutes ago," Jimmy replied. "Can you tell me what the clue is?"

"Of course," Nan said, and quickly told her suspicion.

Jimmy gave a low whistle. "You may have the best lead yet," he praised Nan. "I'll tell Dad as soon as he gets back." Jimmy explained that he was keeping an eye on the trailer until his father's return. Jandy and her mother were in the arena to do a special circus act.

Jimmy agreed with Bert's theory that Gee-Gee's assailant and the safe-cracker were the same person. Questioning among the performers and workmen had been of no help.

"Anyway," Jimmy said, "I hope the mystery's cleared up soon. Many circus people are superstitious. This could be bad for the Happy Top!"

"You mean performers will be afraid to stay with your Dad's show?" Bert put in.

Jimmy admitted this was exactly what might happen.

"That would be dreadful!" Nan exclaimed. She and Bert promised to do all they could to assist the Duncans.

"Thanks." Jimmy smiled. "You're swell friends."

The twins said good-by and returned to their seats. When it was time for Jandy and Carla's act, the Bobbseys leaned forward expectantly. Mother and daughter fairly flew through a series of acrobatic leaps, twirls, and double-flips.

"My goodness gracious!" Dinah exclaimed. "I'm 'most out of breath just watchin' those two!"

"Aren't they marvelous!" Nan cried.

At the end of their stunt the Duncans smiled and waved graciously at the audience, who applauded heartily. Nan thought, "Carla and

Jandy appear so carefree, and yet must be dreadfully worried."

Several entertaining animal features came next. The twins liked one particularly because it reminded them of the missing Waggo. Two frisky terriers pranced around on a large drum, beating it with their tails and paws in time to the band music.

"Drummer dogs," Flossie remarked. "Aren't they smart?"

"If we had Waggo back," Freddie said wistfully, "he could do that with Snap."

When the performance was over, the twins and Dinah hurried home. They found Mr. and Mrs. Bobbsey seated on the porch glider.

"The circus got robbed this afternoon and Nan saw the monkey-headed thief!" Freddie burst out.

"What!" Mr. Bobbsey exclaimed.

"Gracious!" his wife added. "Who was it?"

Nan and Bert quickly told the story. At the end Mr. Bobbsey said, "I'm sure the Lakeport police will find him."

Presently Mrs. Bobbsey smiled, saying, "How would you like to have a picnic supper in the back yard?"

"Yippee!" exclaimed Freddie.

The small twins carried out paper napkins, plates, and tablecloth as well as utensils. Nan and Bert helped Mrs. Bobbsey and Dinah take the food to the rustic table under the big apple tree.

Soon the family were seated on the long benches, eating spiced ham, potato salad, and hot muffins.

"This is a perfect after-the-circus meal," Nan said.

They had scooped-out melon halves, filled with ice cream for dessert. The Bobbseys enjoyed the cool, delicious dessert, then the table was quickly cleared and everything put away.

Nan went to see her friends about the circus act she had in mind. Bert headed for Charlie Mason's house to talk over the boys' stunt. The younger twins stayed in the back yard.

"Let's play in our circus tent," Freddie suggested.

He and Flossie walked inside the tent and sat down on the discarded mattress Sam had brought from the attic.

"I know what we can teach Snoop for his circus act," Freddie said to his twin.

"What?"

"Snoop can be a cat tightrope walker. Even the Happy Top didn't have that!"

Flossie giggled. "A cat-dog! But how do we start?"

For answer Freddie beckoned Flossie to follow him from the tent into the kitchen, where Dinah and Sam were talking.

"Dinah, may we have some clothesline?" Freddie asked.

"I expect so, honey." Dinah chuckled. "You two goin' to play cowboys?"

Freddie and Flossie shook their heads. "We have to practice a special trick," Flossie said. "You'll see it when you come to our circus."

Sam winked at his wife. "Guess we'll have to wait. But I'm sure burstin' with curiosity."

The twins giggled at the thought of lean Sam bursting. Then Dinah gave Freddie a length of line and the children ran outside. Quickly they tied the clothesline around the trunks of two cherry trees about six feet apart.

They found Snoop dozing peacefully underneath a dogwood tree in the back of the yard. "Wake up, kitty," Flossie coaxed. "You're going to learn a new trick that's lots of fun."

Snoop opened one bright eye and looked warily at the twins. Flossie gently picked up her pet, while Freddie dragged the mattress from the tent and placed it beneath the line.

"If Snoop falls, he'll have a soft landing spot," the little boy said. "And the tightrope is only as high as my shoulder."

Then he took Snoop from Flossie and carefully placed the cat's front paws on the end of the taut line.

"Now walk across, Snoop. Go on, boy!"

Flossie bent down, ready to pull the mattress

along beneath the cat. As Snoop's weight rested on the clothesline, it began to sway, even though Freddie still held the pet firmly.

"Snoop," Flossie said, "if you learn this trick you'll be a circus star."

The twins held their breaths as Freddie let go of Snoop. The cat put out a timid paw and

stepped forward. Just then the line jerked downward and Snoop lost his balance.

"Oh!" Flossie gasped.

But instead of slipping off, the black cat clung to the rope. The next second Snoop had flipped underneath and hung there by his claws upside down, swinging from side to side.

The twins stared at their pet in amazement. Then Freddie cheered, "Hoo-ray for Snoop! He did a better stunt than rope walking!"

Flossie agreed. "He's a tumble cat. I hope he'll do it that way for the circus."

"Let's try it again," Freddie urged.

"Maybe if we give Snoop a tidbit, he'll learn faster," Flossie suggested. She dashed into the kitchen and came back with a small dish of chopped liver.

Once more Freddie set the cat onto the rope, and gradually released his hold. "Me-ow!" Snoop put a front paw forward. Again the line sagged, and the cat swung beneath it, clinging tightly.

"Oh wonderful!" Flossie squealed, lifting Snoop and hugging him. She then gave the meat to him. He ate it hungrily.

Meanwhile, Nan had returned home from visiting Grace and Nellie. She was well pleased with the circus routine she and her friends had worked out—a lively and unusual clown dance. "We can make cute costumes, too," she thought eagerly. "Maybe Mother will help me sew them."

Nan went into the living room and consulted Mrs. Bobbsey, who said she would be glad to assist. As they discussed the costumes, a thought suddenly popped into Nan's mind.

"Oh!" she exclaimed.

"What is it, dear?" her mother asked and Mr. Bobbsey looked up from the newspaper he had been reading.

"That clown in the monkey suit! I just remembered he had an odd kind of walk—almost a limp," Nan told her parents.

They both agreed this could be valuable in identifying the person. When Bert returned home, Nan told him about the clue she had overlooked.

"Let's go down to the Happy Top first thing in the morning," Bert urged, "and tell K. T. Duncan."

Nan and Bert were up early the next day. They had a quick breakfast with Mr. Bobbsey. When he left for the lumberyard, the twins rode with him as far as downtown Lakeport. They hopped out of the car and hastened to the circus grounds. When the children arrived they stopped short and cried out in disbelief:

"The Happy Top is gone!"

CHAPTER XVI

A WELCOME VISITOR

CIRCUS tents, stands, trailers, and trucks had vanished! The Happy Top had indeed left Lakeport! Nan and Bert were completely mystified and disappointed.

"It's funny Jandy and Jimmy Duncan didn't tell us they were going to move," Nan said. "The Happy Top was supposed to stay here an extra day."

"Unless they didn't know until late last night," Bert reasoned. "K. T. must have decided to leave all of a sudden."

"Maybe someone can tell us where the circus went." Nan looked around and saw a park groundskeeper trimming hedges.

The twins hurried over to question him. "All I heard," he replied, "is that Duncan's outfit left for Dellmont about four o'clock this morning."

"Do you know why?" Bert asked.

"Well," the park man continued, "I under-

stand there'd been a run o' bad luck at the
Happy Top here. Maybe K. T. figured he'd better get to a new spot where things would be
better."

The twins thanked the park worker and
walked off. Nan remarked with a sigh, "Dellmont's a long way from here. Perhaps we should
tell the Lakeport police about that monkey-
clown's limp."

"Good idea," Bert replied.

He and Nan turned their steps toward headquarters. When they went inside, the twins were
greeted jovially by Chief Smith, an old friend
of the Bobbseys.

"I'm sorry I haven't any news about that missing dog," he told the children.

"We've come to see you about another mystery," Nan said.

The police chief listened intently, then remarked, "This fellow's limp could be an excellent clue. *If* he *is* the thief, it may help catch
him." After a moment's pause, the officer added,
"There's one thing I guess you twins don't know
about the burglary. It was fake money that was
stolen from the safe."

Bert and Nan stared at Chief Smith dum-
founded. "Fake!" they echoed.

The chief nodded. "K. T. had told me about
items missing from the circus, including small
sums of money. I suggested that he set a 'trap'

for the thief by putting a large amount of imitation bills in the safe."

Chief Smith said that the bills looked real enough to fool anyone in a hurry. "The trouble was that the thief came before K. T. expected him to and didn't have a chance to catch him."

"I guess," Bert ventured, "K. T. pretended to be upset so the guilty person wouldn't suspect the truth about the money if he was still around."

"That's correct," the chief replied. He promised to telephone the Dellmont authorities at once and have K. T. notified of Nan's latest clue.

As the children left the station house, Nan said, "I have some shopping to do for *our* circus. 'Bye Bert," she added with a twinkle.

"Oh, a secret, eh? So long, Sis. See you later." With a grin Bert headed toward Charlie Mason's house.

Nan entered a large music store and made a purchase. Then she went to Nellie Parks' home, which was near the Bobbseys'. She rang the bell, and Nellie, blond and pretty, opened the door. "Come on in," her friend cried excitedly. "Grace and I can hardly wait!"

Nan stepped inside and greeted dark-haired Grace Lavine, who also was twelve.

"Hi, Nan!" she said. "Did you get the records?"

Nan smiled, opened her package and held up

three phonograph records. Nellie put them on the player one by one. The first was a soft, sweet Hawaiian melody, the second a haunting gypsy tune, and the third a lively Irish jig.

As Nellie took the last disc from the spindle, Grace said, "They're all lovely, but I think I'll choose the Hawaiian music for my part of our circus dance."

Nellie giggled. "You'll be good as a hula clown." Then she turned to Nan and asked, "Which do you want, the gypsy or the Irish?"

Nan replied she would like to do the gypsy dance.

"That leaves the Irish jig for my number," Nellie said. "I was hoping I'd get it."

The three girls merrily began practicing their dance routines to the music. Finally, after much swaying, whirling, and hopping, they laughingly stopped for breath and sank down on the sofa. The practice went on until almost lunchtime. Then Nan and Grace bade Nellie good-by and left for their homes.

When Nan walked into her back yard, she found Bert and Charlie practicing stunts on the old mattress. Freddie and Flossie were watching.

"Hi, Nan!" Charlie called. He was kneeling on the mattress, with Bert crouched on his friend's shoulders.

"Watch this!" Bert said. Slowly and care-

fully, with Charlie gripping his ankles, Bert
stood up. "All set?" he cried. "Here I go!"

Bert leaped to the mattress and turned a double somersault. At the same moment Charlie did
a cartwheel. The two boys jumped to a standing
position together.

"Wonderful!" Nan clapped vigorously.
"You boys will be a hit!"

When the twins went into the house to have

lunch, Mrs. Bobbsey met them in the kitchen. Her blue eyes were twinkling as she said, "We have a surprise luncheon guest."

"How 'citing!" cried Flossie. "Who?"

Her mother motioned toward the living room. Eagerly the twins hurried in and exclaimed in delight. Sandy Blaine jumped up from a chair to greet them.

"Did you ride here on Cockles?" Freddie asked.

"Oh my, no!" Sandy laughed merrily.

She explained that Mrs. Bobbsey had telephoned Mrs. Blaine at the farm to see when Sandy might visit the twins. Today had been decided upon, since her grandfather had to drive to Lakeport with some farm produce. He would return early that afternoon to pick her up.

Dinah entered the living room and gave Sandy a big smile. "Lunch is ready. Hope you're real hungry, Sandy."

"I certainly am, Dinah," the visitor declared.

Everyone was in gay spirits as the group sat down at the table. Dinah served broiled hamburgers and home-baked beans with a crisp apple salad. The children chatted and joked throughout the delicious meal.

When it was over, Mrs. Bobbsey suggested they have dessert—milk shakes and gingerbread—on the side porch. "It's cool and shady there," she added.

When the Bobbseys and their young guest were seated on the porch, Nan asked about Sandy's mother.

"She's much better," Sandy replied. "We had a note from her saying she'll be able to come to the farm soon." The girl's face clouded. "But I haven't heard from Daddy yet."

Mrs. Bobbsey reminded Sandy that her father was probably waiting until he found a position before writing. The circus girl nodded but still looked grave.

"Perhaps," she replied. "It's not like Daddy to worry us, though."

"We saw the Happy Top Circus," Freddie spoke up, hoping to make Sandy feel better. She did brighten, and asked the twins for details.

They took turns telling of the parade, the performances, the Duncans, and other Happy Top people they had met, and finally of Gee-Gee's accident and the robbing of K. T.'s safe.

"Ha ha!" Freddie laughed. "I'll bet that thief'll be mad when he discovers he stole fake money."

Sandy nodded, then said, "The circus we worked for out West had a robbery too."

"When was that?" Bert asked.

Sandy said the robbery had occurred the night her mother had fallen from the trapeze. While the manager of the circus had been investigating her mother's accident, several hundred dollars had been stolen from his office safe. The police had been called in but the thief had never been caught.

"And not only that," Sandy added. "When my mother regained consciousness in the hospital, she discovered a valuable opal ring she had been wearing was missing."

"How dreadful!" Nan cried sympathetically. "You think the ring was taken?"

Sandy nodded sadly. "I'm afraid so. Dad thought probably someone slipped it off her finger while she was unconscious, before the doctor came. There was such a crowd around, the person wasn't noticed."

At this moment Mr. Bobbsey walked onto the porch.

"Daddy, you're home early," Flossie exclaimed, hugging him.

The twins' father smiled. "I have a special reason." Nan introduced him to Sandy Blaine.

"I'm glad to know you, Sandy," Mr. Bobbsey said, then looked around at the group. "Who wants to go on a trip with me?" he asked.

"I do!" shouted the four twins at once, and Mrs. Bobbsey laughingly added, "So do I. Where to, Dick?"

Her husband replied that he must discuss a lumber contract in a mountain resort town two hundred miles away. "A place called Dellmont."

"Dellmont!" Bert echoed excitedly. "That's where the Happy Top Circus went!"

His father was surprised to hear this; he had not known of the circus's departure.

"Well," Mr. Bobbsey said, "this will be a business-vacation-circus-mystery trip. We'll stay at the Holiday Motel in Dellmont. They have a swimming pool and a riding stable on the grounds."

"It sounds wonderful!" Nan said. She glanced at Sandy Blaine, who had a wistful expression in her eyes. As Mr. Bobbsey walked back into the house Nan followed him. "Daddy, could Sandy come with us?" she asked.

"Of course, if she'd like to and her folks say it's all right," Mr. Bobbsey replied. "There's plenty of room in our station wagon." He returned to the porch and gave the invitation.

"Oh, Mr. Bobbsey, I'd love to!" Sandy cried, her eyes sparkling now.

A short while later Mr. Blaine arrived in the farm truck. Sandy introduced her grandfather and asked permission to go on the trip.

"Why, it's sure nice of you Bobbseys to include Sandy," the farmer said. "Certainly she may go."

"Then we'll stop for Sandy at nine tomorrow morning," Mr. Bobbsey said.

Later that afternoon the twins had another meeting in their back yard with the six friends who were to be in the home circus. Bob Glade, a boy of eleven, was put in charge of making posters to be displayed around town. Charlie Mason offered to print admission tickets. Teddy Blake and Susie Larker, a friend of Flossie's, offered to collect them at the circus "gate."

"And we'll all sell as many tickets as we can," Nan spoke up.

"Yes," Flossie put in. "We'll make lots of money for Campers' Corner."

"And we'll keep on practicing our acts," promised Grace Lavine, as she did a dance step on the grass. The others agreed, and wished the twins a good trip, but a quick return for the home circus.

At eight-thirty next day the family started for the Blaine farm. Sandy and her grandmother were waiting on the front porch. They hurried down the steps and Bert put Sandy's suitcase with the other baggage.

"I certainly appreciate your taking Sandy along," Mrs. Blaine told Mr. and Mrs. Bobbsey, adding in a lower tone, "She's been a bit lonesome without playmates. The twins have cheered her immensely."

"We're all very fond of Sandy," Mrs. Bobbsey said, smiling. "I'm so glad she'll be with us."

The circus girl kissed Mrs. Blaine good-by. "Please tell Cockles I'll be back soon, Grandma."

"I will, dear. Have fun."

Sandy climbed into the middle seat beside Nan and Flossie. The children, in a joyful mood, sang one rollicking tune after another as they rode through the countryside. Sandy seemed to be enjoying herself tremendously. Later, the twins told their new friend the latest plans for their circus.

Suddenly Flossie said, "It's going to rain. How black the sky is getting!"

As she spoke, huge drops of rain splattered on the windshield.

"Better close the windows," Mr. Bobbsey said. "We're in for a real cloudburst."

No sooner were the windows rolled up than there came a deafening crash of thunder, followed by a jagged streak of lightning. Sheets of water poured from the sky.

In a few minutes Mr. Bobbsey turned off the main highway onto a narrow road where a sign pointed to Dellmont. As the intensity of the rain increased, it became extremely difficult to see ahead.

"Let's pull over to the side until the storm stops," Mrs. Bobbsey suggested.

Her husband started to do so. All of a sudden the tires skidded on a muddy patch and the car swerved violently.

"Watch out, Dad!" Bert shouted. "We're headed for a ditch!"

CHAPTER XVII

FOUND!

FOR a moment the Bobbseys thought they would plunge into the roadside ditch. Just in time, Mr. Bobbsey regained control of the car and gently applied the brakes. He drove slowly to a point beyond the ditch, then pulled over to the side and turned off the ignition.

"Phew!" he exclaimed. "That was a close one!" Mr. Bobbsey mopped his brow. "Good thing you noticed that ditch, Bert," he said, and inquired if everyone was all right.

The children and Mrs. Bobbsey said that outside of being a bit shaky from their scare they were fine. Soon the rain stopped and Mr. Bobbsey started off once more.

Presently Freddie announced, "I'm awful hungry."

Mrs. Bobbsey smiled. "I guess we all are. It *is* lunchtime."

The travelers kept their eyes open for a good

place to eat. A few miles farther on they rounded a turn in the road and saw an attractive restaurant called "The Country Garden." Mr. Bobbsey pulled into the parking lot, which was surrounded by holly hedges, lovely roses, and larkspur.

"This really *is* a country garden," Mrs. Bobbsey remarked.

After enjoying delicious chicken sandwiches, milk, and chocolate eclairs, the travelers went on their way to Dellmont again. About an hour later, Mr. Bobbsey turned the station wagon into a winding, shrub-lined drive—the entrance to the Holiday Motel.

"Say, this is keen!" Bert exclaimed, glancing around the spacious grounds.

The Holiday was a ranch-style motel with individual family units and carports. The buildings were painted a sunshine yellow and trimmed with sparkling white. Off to one side was a large restaurant and a swimming pool. A sign read, "Riding horses in the rear."

"It'll be fun staying here," Flossie remarked as Mr. Bobbsey stopped the car before the registration office. Everyone got out and waited while the twins' father went inside the office.

Presently he came outside with the manager who led the group to their unit. It had three bedrooms, baths, and a homey living room with yellow leather furniture.

"I'm so glad you asked me to come!" Sandy said, as Bert helped Mr. Bobbsey carry in the bags.

"We are too!" Flossie replied.

The girls could see the pool from their window. The blue-green water looked inviting, and Nan suggested they go for a swim.

"Oh, let's!" Flossie agreed eagerly and the girls put on their bathing suits. When they arrived at the pool, they found Bert and Freddie already in the water.

"Last one in is a water buffalo!" shouted Freddie, and Flossie made a beeline for the low diving board.

With a loud *whee-ee* Flossie flopped into the water feet first. Sandy, followed by Nan, dived in. A few minutes later Mr. and Mrs. Bobbsey, too, joined the children for a swim.

A little later Freddie noticed an assortment of large water toys near the pool. Next to them was a sign. "For our young guests to use— Holiday Motel."

"Oh boy!" Freddie shouted.

It was not long before the twins and Sandy had each selected a toy in a fish or animal shape. Sandy grinned as she sat astride her red-and-blue rubber horse.

"First time I've ever gone riding in the water."

Bert chuckled. "At least, falling off won't

hurt," he joked, pushing himself along on a purple porpoise with green eyes.

"I know!" Flossie bounced up and down on her green and pink spotted water "leopard." "Let's have a race across the pool."

Instantly the five young racers lined up where Mr. and Mrs. Bobbsey were seated at the pool's edge. Nan asked her parents to be referees.

"All right." Mr. Bobbsey stood up. "On your mark—get set—go!"

Paddling their feet and hands furiously, the children splashed through the water atop their rubber mounts.

"Come on, you slowpoke!" Freddie urged his yellow-and-black whale. He was behind the others. The little boy leaned forward and pushed extra hard with his arms. Suddenly he lost his balance and toppled off.

"Oh-oh, you're out!" Flossie called to her twin as he sputtered and laughed at the same time.

Finally Bert and Sandy were the only ones still in the race. Flossie's leopard and Nan's red turtle had tipped over, spilling the girls into the water. Amidst giggling, they cheered first Sandy, then Bert. As the pair approached the other side, Sandy pulled ahead by half an inch and brought her horse in first.

Mr. Bobbsey announced with a broad smile, "Sandy Blaine wins! Bert Bobbsey, second place."

"Hurray!" Freddie shouted, and everyone agreed it had been the funniest—and slowest race ever.

Nan, Flossie, and Sandy climbed from the pool, put on beach robes and slippers, and said they were going to look for the riding stables.

They headed for the rear of the property. The horse barn was located in a little grove. A lean, tanned groom with a friendly face was sweeping out the stables.

"Hi there!" he greeted the girls. "I'm Tad Hopper. Like to have a look around?"

"Oh yes," Sandy said eagerly.

The trio entered the low building, which smelled of sweet hay. There were a dozen stalls containing sleek brown horses and several Shetland ponies.

"This one reminds me of Cockles!" Sandy said happily, as a friendly Shetland nuzzled her hand.

Nan and Flossie stroked the pony. "Yes," Nan remarked. "He could be Cockles' brother."

When the trio walked outside the stable, they saw a small black-and-white dog asleep underneath a nearby willow tree. The Bobbsey girls stared at him in astonishment.

"Waggo!" cried Nan and Flossie. The next instant they were thunderstruck to hear Sandy yell, "Chips!"

The black-and-white terrier awoke and leaped forward with a joyous bark. Sandy ran to meet him, saying "Chips! Chips!"

Nan and Flossie had stopped in their tracks and were looking at each other, mystified. Chips was the name Mr. Riker had called the dog. Did Sandy know Mr. Riker? And what was the terrier doing way out here?

"You've seen this dog before, Sandy?" Nan finally managed to say, as she and Flossie went up to pat the terrier.

Sandy nodded excitedly. "Of course! Chips belongs to my father and was with him when

Daddy went away." Her face grew pale as she added, "Why, that must mean Daddy is near here!"

Nan's mind was racing. She remembered that Sandy had said her father had red hair. Mr. Riker was also red-haired. Were they one and the same person?

"Do you know the name 'Riker'?" Nan asked aloud.

"Why yes," Sandy said in surprise. She explained that this was the name her parents had used at the circus. It had been her mother's maiden name. "My folks were always known as 'The Flying Rikers,' " Sandy declared proudly.

"Then we've met your father, Sandy!" Flossie blurted out.

Nan related the whole story to the bewildered girl starting with the time Mr. Riker had almost run over Snap, to Waggo's abrupt disappearance from the Bobbsey home.

When she had finished, Sandy's eyes filled with tears. "But if Dad was in Lakeport last week, why didn't he come out to the farm?" she asked.

Nan was quick to assure her there must have been a good reason. "We'll tell my Dad all about it," she said. "He might help solve the mystery."

Flossie had been turning her head in every direction. Now she spoke up. "Maybe the bad person who took Waggo from us is here at this motel!"

"You're right, Floss," Nan agreed. "Let's find out."

The girls had gone barely five steps when Waggo gave a bark and dashed toward a boy who was walking toward them.

Nan gasped. "Jack Westly!" she cried, noting in astonishment that Waggo had run over to Jack and was licking his hand! The boy patted the dog's head.

"Jack, do *you* know Waggo too?" Flossie asked incredulously.

"Sure I do. But his name is Bingo and he belongs to me now!" Jack replied, scowling. "So you Bobbseys leave my dog alone."

Nan and Flossie were speechless. How had the terrier come into the possession of Danny Rugg's pal?

Despite this perplexing situation, Flossie could not help giggling. Now the black-and-white terrier had three names—Chips, Waggo, and Bingo!

At this point Sandy demanded of Jack, "What do you mean, *your* dog Bingo? He belongs to my father! Here Chips!"

Immediately the terrier bounded to Sandy's side and jumped up playfully. A furious expression crossed Jack's face.

Nan hastily introduced the two children, then said, "Sandy's right, Jack. We met her father while he was looking for Chips."

The boy laughed scornfully. "Huh! I don't believe it. Besides, I bought this dog myself from Danny—" He broke off as if fearing he had said too much.

"You *bought* Waggo from Danny *Rugg?*" Nan cried.

Just then Bert and Freddie hurried across the lawn and joined the group. Both boys were amazed and overjoyed to see Waggo, who greeted them affectionately, his tail wagging violently.

"Hi!" Bert said to Jack who stood by sullenly.

Nan told her brothers Sandy's story, then of Jack's claiming the black-and-white dog. "Jack says he bought Waggo from Danny," she concluded.

"What!" echoed Bert and Freddie.

Jack glared at the group defiantly for a moment.

"Better tell us what happened," Bert said firmly.

Glumly the other boy replied that his pal had seen Waggo leaving the Bobbseys' home carrying a meat bone. Then, according to Danny he had heard Dinah say, "And don't you come back!" So Danny had whistled to the terrier, who followed him home.

"Dinah never said that," Freddie interrupted vehemently. "We were right there." The other twins nodded.

"Anyway, Danny kept the dog in his cellar overnight," Jack continued, "but Bingo ran away the next day."

"And came back to us," Flossie broke in.

"But didn't someone take my daddy's dog from your yard?" Sandy asked the twins.

"Yes," they chorused.

Jack flushed. "I don't know anything about that. Danny just told me he found Bingo again, but his mother wouldn't let him keep a dog. So he sold Bingo to me for five dollars."

"Some nerve!" Bert cried hotly.

"How long have you been at the Holiday Motel, Jack?" Nan asked.

"My folks and I came Sunday," the boy said, and the Bobbseys remembered this was the day after Waggo had disappeared.

Sandy and the older twins wondered what to do next. They realized Jack had bought the pet, not knowing that he belonged to someone else.

"I'll bet," Freddie spoke up, "Danny *was* the one who gave Waggo the meat to get him away that night."

"M-meat?" stammered Jack.

"Yes. Chopped meat," Bert told the boy. "We found some on a piece of waxed paper near the dog run."

"So that's why Danny bought some chopped —" Jack stopped short, suddenly realizing that the Bobbseys' suspicions of Danny were correct.

"Okay, Jack," Bert said. "You know now this dog doesn't really belong to you *or* us."

For a long moment Jack looked at the ground. Then he stroked the terrier and said gruffly to Sandy, "Take back your father's dog." He turned and stalked away.

"Poor Jack," Nan sighed. "Besides losing Waggo—I mean—Chips—he's learned his best friend told him a lie."

With the black-and-white terrier prancing beside them, the children returned to the motel. Mr. and Mrs. Bobbsey were amazed to see the missing pet. And the twins' parents were astounded to learn that Mr. Riker was Sandy Blaine's father. Mr. Bobbsey promised that if no word had been received from Sandy's father by the time they returned to Lakeport, he would make an investigation.

"But I have a feeling you'll see your daddy soon," Mrs. Bobbsey told the circus girl.

This seemed to cheer Sandy considerably. Mr. Bobbsey, his eyes twinkling, said:

"I understand the Happy Top is giving its Dellmont performance tomorrow. Would everyone like to see the show?"

"Goody!" "Swell." "You bet." "Love to," the twins responded together.

Sandy, her green eyes sparkling like emeralds, asked, "And it's all right for me to go, too?"

Mrs. Bobbsey smilingly nodded, saying she had phoned Sandy's grandfather and he had given permission. The twins' mother would go with the children while Mr. Bobbsey attended to his lumber deal.

"It'll be fun to see the Duncans again!" Nan exclaimed.

"And we can find out about the circus thief!" Freddie added. "Maybe he's been caught."

Next day directly after lunch the Bobbseys and Sandy climbed into the station wagon. Sandy held Chips on her lap. On the way to the circus grounds Mr. Bobbsey got out at an office building where he had his business appointment.

A short time later, Mrs. Bobbsey drew into a lot near the Happy Top site and parked the car. Chips was left inside the car and the others alighted. At the gate the twins' mother bought tickets and everyone entered the circus area and looked around.

"It's just like home," Sandy exclaimed, her face glowing with excitement.

The Bobbseys led her to the side show tent, then the menagerie tent. The twins were greeted with friendly waves from the circus people they had met before.

"It's time to go to our seats," Bert said presently. And the group went into the bleachers.

Soon the show started with the blare of trumpets and the Grand Entry Parade. Sandy was enthralled and the twins, who never tired of the circus, said it was as "good as ever."

As the clowns came into the arena, Freddie tugged at Bert's shirt sleeve. "I'm real thirsty," he said. "I'd like a glass of water."

Bert laughed and told his mother they would go to a water fountain he had seen near the main gate. Flossie wanted to come too.

The three children hurried outside. The grounds there were deserted. As the Bobbseys started toward the water fountain, Freddie stopped short.

"Smell the air!" he exclaimed. "Something's burning!"

There was a strange, pungent aroma which the children had not noticed at first.

"I smell it, too," Flossie said, sniffing.

Freddie's eyes popped. "A fire!" he cried. "Quick! Let's find it!"

"If only you had your fire engine, Freddie," Flossie panted, as the children made a hasty survey of the surrounding area.

They approached a field behind the menagerie tent. Suddenly Bert halted. "Look!" he cried, pointing.

Straight ahead, close to the tent, a huge pile

of rags and wooden boards was a blazing mass
of flames!

"Oh dear!" cried Flossie. "The Happy Top
might burn down again!"

"Quick!" Bert said. "We must give the
alarm!"

CHAPTER XVIII

THE BEST REWARD

AS Flossie and Freddie stared at the flames leaping closer to the menagerie tent, Bert rushed inside. He saw an attendant and yelled:

"Get help! There's a fire out back!"

Immediately the man dashed about, summoning assistance. Workmen grabbed fire extinquishers and ran outside. As the Bobbseys started to follow them, Bert saw Nan hurrying inside the tent.

"Here you are!" she cried, rushing up. Breathlessly she explained that Mrs. Bobbsey had become worried when the three had not returned. Nan had offered to find them.

Quickly Bert told about the dangerous blaze and Freddie urged, "Let's watch the fire fighters!"

Nan was dismayed, but had news of her own. "Bert," she said, "I just saw that clown with the limping walk. He was heading for K. T.'s trailer! I'll bet he's going to try robbing the safe again."

Bert snapped his fingers. "And I'll bet he's the one who set the fire, to get everybody away from the trailer."

Bert told Nan and the younger twins to look for K. T. Duncan. Perhaps the circus owner had been notified of the fire and was already at the scene. "I'll go after that fake clown," Bert declared.

"All right," Nan agreed. "But be careful."

As the other twins hurried off, Bert raced toward the main gate. Every person he passed was running toward the menagerie tent. Word of the fire must have spread rapidly, the boy thought. The area near the office trailer was deserted.

Quietly Bert went up to one of the trailer windows. Peering in, he saw that the door of K. T.'s safe stood open. Crouched on the floor in front of it was a clown gaudily dressed in a purple-and-orange suit. The clown was stuffing money into a large bag!

"What shall I do?" thought Bert, knowing that if he shouted an alarm, the thief might bolt from the trailer. Then too, at the moment there was no one to come to his aid.

"And maybe it's not imitation money he's taking this time," Bert told himself.

Suddenly he spotted a long piece of rope ly-

ing underneath the trailer. It gave him an idea
Picking up the rope, Bert crept over to the door

First he carefully secured the rope in a tight
knot on the door handle, and then attached the
other end to the trailer axle. With the rope
pulled taut it would be impossible to open the
door from inside.

At this moment Gee-Gee the clown, K. T.
Duncan, Nan, Flossie, and Freddie came running toward the trailer. As they came up, Freddie cried, "The fire's out, Bert—"

He was interrupted by a loud pounding on
the trailer door. An enraged clown's face appeared at a window.

"That's the thief!" Bert told K. T. "I saw him taking money from your safe."

"Good work, Bert!" K. T. praised the boy and Gee-Gee added, "Inside that trailer you've trapped one of the slickest crooks in the country."

"You know who he is?" Bert asked in surprise.

K. T. answered grimly, "Gee-Gee and I are pretty certain we know. We've had our suspicions for some time, but not enough proof. Thanks to you, Bert, and your brother and sisters' help, we'll find out right now."

Everyone waited tensely as Gee-Gee untied the rope and K. T. opened the trailer door.

"Come on out!" he ordered sternly. "We've got you surrounded."

Two stalwart circus workmen hurried to his side. Finally, a tall figure in purple and orange emerged from the trailer. Immediately the men seized him by his arms.

"Let go o' me—you got nothin' on me!" the thief in clown's costume snarled.

K. T. Duncan eyed the man coldly and said, "You have just been seen taking money from my safe. We have evidence you've taken other things. I'm going to phone the police."

He hurried into the trailer. In a few minutes he returned to report that a squad car was being dispatched.

Meanwhile, Flossie had been watching the

tall clown. "Why, he's wearing a mask instead of grease paint, K. T.!" she exclaimed.

"And false-bottom shoes," Nan pointed out, noticing that the heels on the man's shoes were about four inches high. This had given him the strange, limping walk.

"Take off that rubber mask and hat, you rascal!" K. T. commanded. Reluctantly the captive obeyed, revealing close-cropped gray hair and a slightly bent nose.

The twins gasped in startled recognition. "It's Amos, the elephant-trainer!" Bert cried out.

At that moment Mrs. Bobbsey and Sandy rushed up. Gee-Gee took one look at Sandy Blaine and his mouth opened with surprise.

"Sandy!" he cried out joyously.

For a second the girl's face turned so pale every freckle seemed to stand out. Then she rushed into the clown's outstretched arms.

"Daddy! Oh, Daddy, I thought you were lost!" she half sobbed.

Everything was in confusion for the next few minutes as father and daughter hugged each other. Finally K. T. motioned his helpers to disperse the gathering crowd.

The twins and their mother had stood back watching in amazement and happiness for Sandy. Nan now said, "Gee-Gee, it's hard to believe you're the Mr. Riker we met that day you were looking for Chips."

Bert agreed, although he remembered that the clown's eyes *had* looked familiar. Sandy Blaine's father grinned, swept off his peaked hat, and pointed to his shock of red hair. "I'll bet," he said, "you Bobbseys would have recognized me without my hat."

For the first time Sandy saw the captured elephant-trainer, who stood sullenly between two husky guards.

"Why, Daddy," she cried, "what's Amos Hammer doing here!"

The twins looked at the girl in surprise. "Have you met Amos before?" Nan asked her.

Sandy nodded, then Mr. Blaine said, "I guess I'd better explain the whole story."

"Please do," Mrs. Bobbsey said.

She and the twins learned that Amos had worked for the same western circus that the Blaines had. At first he had been the head animal-trainer, but the circus-owner had caught him being cruel to the animals. So he had demoted Amos to general handyman.

Mr. Blaine went on to say that he and others at the circus had suspected Amos of not being trustworthy. Moreover, when Sandy's mother, Rusty, had fallen from the trapeze, Amos was in the arena. He had been among the first to reach her side. When Rusty had regained consciousness, she had discovered that her beautiful opal ring was missing.

"Your circus was robbed that same night, too!" Nan spoke up, remembering Sandy's story.

Mr. Blaine nodded, saying that since Amos had disappeared immediately after that theft, he had been suspected. But the police had not been able to locate the former trainer.

Sandy could not keep silent any longer. "Daddy, why didn't you tell me you were working for the Happy Top Circus?"

Her father explained that he had come to Lakeport for a job interview the day he had lost Chips and met the Bobbseys. At that point the children told him what had happened to Chips in the meantime.

"And, Daddy," Sandy concluded, "he's safe outside in the Bobbseys' car."

"That's wonderful news!" Mr. Blaine exclaimed.

He resumed his own story, "It was at the gasoline station where Chips ran away that I saw Amos Hammer. He was buying kerosene. I decided then and there to follow him and find out the truth. The trail led to the Happy Top in Marymont, and I learned Amos worked for the circus.

"I went to see K. T., and asked for a temporary job as a clown, so I could keep an eye on Amos. That's why I didn't stop at the farm first, Sandy, or get in touch with you."

K. T. smiled. "You didn't tell me about your

suspicions of Amos, though, until the day he struck you in the arena."

"Did Amos find out who you were?" Bert put in.

"No," Mr. Blaine replied. "I made sure he never saw me without my brown wig and the grease paint on my face. He knocked me out, I'm sure, to pay me back because I'd caught him stealing a clown suit from the wardrobe tent."

At this, Amos Hammer growled, "If I'd known it was you in that get-up, I'd have scrammed out of town."

K. T. Duncan then related how, in Lakeport, he and Gee-Gee had carried out the plan for catching Amos. They had planted fake money in the safe. Then they had let word get around the circus that many thousands of dollars were there.

The circus-owner turned to Nan. "And, as you know, our scheme almost worked. Jimmy told me you had spotted a fellow in a monkey outfit near my office. Yesterday I heard through the police about his odd walk."

"Why did you leave for Dellmont a day early?" Bert asked.

With a sigh K. T. admitted that he had been persuaded to move on because the performers had become very nervous after the theft.

"Some of my people," he went on, "were sure they'd give a better show in a new spot." He threw Amos Hammer a wry glance. "And you put on a big act yourself, saying our luck would change in Dellmont."

The Bobbseys and Sandy also learned that Amos had come to K. T. with letters saying he was an honest workman. "However," K. T. declared, "I think now you wrote them yourself."

Amos admitted he had. He also confessed that he had caused the first fire in Marymont with the kerosene he had bought in Lakeport. And he had been responsible for the blaze behind the menagerie tent.

Further questioning revealed that the man had stolen equipment and costumes, weakened tent poles by sawing partway through them, and had let the lion and cubs out of their cages.

"But why?" Nan queried.

"Because," Amos said sullenly, "I wanted to get the Happy Top for myself. I thought if Duncan got tired of so much bad luck, he'd sell me his circus cheap."

Just then the police arrived and took charge of the thief. As they were about to lead Amos Hammer away, Mr. Blaine said, "There's one other thing—what about my wife's opal ring?"

"Here," the ex-trainer replied curtly. Reaching into his pants pocket, he brought out his wallet. Wrapped in tissue paper was the lovely ring. He handed it to Sandy, then the police escorted him away.

"I'm so glad we've found Mother's ring," said Sandy, hugging her father. "We must let her know you're here, so she won't worry."

Mr. Blaine confided that his wife and parents too, had known all the time of his plan. But they had decided that it was best not to tell Sandy for a while, at least.

"I was afraid, honey," he said to his daughter, "if you came to the circus, you might give away my disguise."

"I probably would have," Sandy laughed.

The girl's happiness was made complete when her father announced he had just received word that his wife Rusty was well enough to travel. "And," he added, "when your mother arrives, Sandy, we're all going to live on father's farm."

The Bobbseys were delighted to hear this. K. T. grinned and said he would miss "Gee-Gee" the clown. "I understand, though," he said, his eyes twinkling, "you have something else lined up."

"Oh Daddy," Sandy burst out, "you *did* find another job!"

"Yes," he replied. "As a result of the interview I had in Lakeport, I'm to be recreation director for Campers' Corner when it opens this summer."

"Campers' Corner!" the twins chorused, and Flossie explained about their project to earn money for the camp by giving a back-yard circus.

"Say, that's great!" Mr. Blaine exclaimed.

"But, what'll you do when camp closes?" Flossie asked him.

"Rusty, Sandy, and I are going to train Shetland ponies for the circus," he replied, adding that a half dozen ponies were already on their way to the farm.

"Oh, Daddy, how wonderful!" Sandy's face glowed. "The three of us will be a team, and I won't have to leave my best friends, the Bobbseys."

"Maybe," Nan said with a smile, "you could help us with our circus, Sandy."

"I'd love to!"

At that moment Carla, Jandy, and Jimmy Duncan rushed up, still in costume. They had just finished performing in the main ring when they had heard about the robbery.

After hearing the whole story, Jandy threw her arms around Nan and Flossie. "How lucky for us that we met the Bobbseys!" she cried, as Carla and Jimmy beamed in gratitude.

K. T. smiled broadly and said, "I'd like to present something to the twins for their project, Campers' Corner. I'm going to donate swings, see-saws, and other circus playthings which children can use."

His offer was greeted with pleased cheers

from the Bobbseys and the Blaines. Sandy's father turned to the twins and announced:

"My daughter and I want to give you twins a token of our appreciation—a token you've named Waggo."

For a moment the Bobbseys could hardly believe their ears.

"To stay with us always ever after?" Flossie cried.

"Yes," Sandy said, "if you want him."

"Do we want him! Oh boy!" Freddie dashed off and was back in a minute with Waggo. "We'll have him in our circus!"

The terrier proved to be one of the hits of the Bobbseys' show. In fact, all the children received loud applause from the onlookers who crowded the tent. Many who could not get in demanded a second performance.

"Everybody said it was bee-yoo-tiful!" Flossie declared later, and Bert, Nan, and Freddie agreed.

"And we made lots of money for the summer camp," Freddie added proudly.

Suddenly Waggo gave a happy bark and turned a backflip. Then the terrier drummed his tail against the floor: *Rat-a-tat-tat! Rat-a-tat-tat!*

It seemed to the Bobbsey twins that Waggo was saying, "I loved it too! And I love it here!"